EDGE:
EAST WIND IN PARADISE

by
Carl Jackson

BOE
BOE
CREATIVE

Boeboe Creative Inc.

Toronto

This book is a work of fiction. Names, characters, businesses, organizations, places, events and incidents either are the product of the author's imagination or are used fictitiously. Any resemblance to actual persons, living or dead, events or locales is entirely coincidental.

Copyright © 2014 by Carl Jackson

All rights reserved. Published by Boeboe Creative Inc.

No part of this book may be reproduced, stored in a retrieval system, or transmitted, in any form or by any means, without written permission of the publisher.

www.shannonedge.com

ISBN: 978-0-9936655-2-3

Cover design by Vaughn Joseph

Contents

Chapter		Page
1.	Death in the Rain	7
2.	The Last of the Rum	15
3.	Hydrofoil Cowboy	24
4.	Coffee Break	32
5.	The Prophet	38
6.	Body Heat	44
7.	Flash Point	49
8.	Hunting Leopards	58
9.	Limbo	63
10.	The Knife Artist	71
11.	Prometheus X	82
12.	The McCool Woman	91
13.	Eagle In The Sky	106
14.	Down-Beat	119

*To My Mother
and Father*

Chapter 1

Death in the Rain

The door to the Broken Spur opened and a policeman came in. He nodded to the barman and leaned against the bar, and his eyes swept over the early afternoon drinkers.

Edward Longstreet saw the policeman, and a chill wind touched the back of his neck. The two men at the table in front of him stopped talking. They had been going on about the Dallas Cowboys and that team's chances of making the Super Bowl. Longstreet passed his hand over his eyes. When he looked again, the policeman was gone.

"Something wrong?" It was the woman sitting with him.

Longstreet looked up from his beer. He had forgotten the woman.

"Thinking," he said. "Just thinking."

"Ready to go now?" she asked.

He studied the face across the table. He wondered what he was doing in a place like this with someone like her. The red-painted lips peeled back and he saw the tobacco-stained teeth. She fluttered her lashes and tossed her head back and swung her heavy blonde hair from side to side. He felt sorry for her. He motioned to her across the table. She came and sat on his knee.

"Do something for me, Sweetheart," he said.

She was smiling at him again. He reached down and drew the envelope out of the top of his boot. He placed it in her bag.

"What's that?" she asked.

"Post this for me," he said. "Don't worry about the stamp. Just drop it in the first mailbox you see."

"What's going on?" She raised an eyebrow and looked him in the eye. "Is everything o.k.?"

"This is important," Longstreet said. "Don't let me down. I'll meet you at your place later."

He gave her twenty dollars. She put the money in her purse and got up off his knee.

"All right," she said. "But don't be long." She kissed him.

He gave her ten minutes, then got up and walked slowly towards the front door. He paused just before reaching the door, turned quickly and walked out the back way. Nobody followed him. He stepped out into the alley. He skirted a pile of garbage and roused a cloud of flies. He heard rats.

It had been a straight-forward assignment, a routine 'observe and report'. He had got the information the agency wanted, but somewhere along the line his cover had been blown. They were hunting him. Nobody had told him, he just knew it. He had to get out fast.

The name of the town was Kingsville. Longstreet hated it. Under the noise and the neon, it was just another grubby Texas town caught in the grip of the economic downturn that seemed to be everywhere. It had been holding its breath for a long time. He grinned sourly. Five years as Eastern Caribbean Station Chief, three months on a desk in Langley, Virginia, and now this. I deserved a better assignment, he thought.

They were waiting for him around the corner. He had been right after all. The policeman had fingered him, and they had covered both exits. He wondered who had paid the policeman. He shook his head. It didn't matter now.

The two men flicked their wrists and he saw the knives. Punks, he thought. I came all this way to die on some punk's knife. He chopped down on a wrist causing the knife to drop. His boot smashed into a groin. A knife ripped him open from belt-buckle to breast-bone.

Shannon Edge lay on his stomach studying the sea through night glasses. Dressed in black with an automatic rifle by his side he scanned the sky, beach and surf around him. He put the glasses down beside the automatic rifle.

There were three of them in the little cove by the cliff. Meyers lay in the sand covering the other side of the beach. Greene waited among the rocks at the foot of the cliff. Edge had told him to keep his head down and call Hervey if anything went wrong.

A sudden cold wind whipped in off the water. Edge pulled the collar of his coat up around his ears. The rain that had been threatening all night started pelting down. He wiped the water from his face and took up the glasses.

The boat came in slowly, hugging the heavier darkness of the shoreline. Edge counted five men.

"Damn it," Edge swore softly. He put down the glasses.

"There was only supposed to be one man," whispered Meyers into his headset.

A man was kneeling in the bow of the boat studying the shore through glasses. Somebody cut the engine and the boat drifted silently towards the shore. The men got out and hauled the boat onto the sand. Edge waited until they were on the beach.

"Stay where you are and put your hands up," he called quietly.

For about the space of four seconds the murmur of the sea was the only sound, then the inlet shook with the thunder of automatic weapons and a stream of fire poured into the rocks around Edge. The group broke into five separate shadows and raced for the shelter of the cliff. Meyers was firing into the darkness as bullets whizzed past him. Edge heard the snarling, trip hammer beat of his American M.16 above the chatter of the Czech-made guns. One of the shadows fell as another continued its quest for the cliff. Edge ran across the beach and dove behind a dune while firing his weapon. Two more shadows crumpled into the sand as gunfire continued to echo through the cove. One of the men raced to the cliff firing wildly behind him. A final burst of automatic fire cut across the beach striking the man in the back and knocking him off of his feet. Meyers knelt in the sand with his weapon still trained on the fallen figure.

Edge searched the sea again. It was empty. He lowered his glasses and walked to where Meyers stood over one of the men. Meyers knelt and shone the torch down on him shielding the light with his hand. The man was dead. He had been cut almost in two. They approached the other bodies warily. Dead men had killed before. They need not have bothered. The five bodies were sprawled on the sand like puppets with broken strings.

And Hervey wanted them alive, Edge thought. But how do you shoot to wound with an automatic weapon when it's the middle of the night, and you're outnumbered and the other guys are shooting back and it's raining and you're scared as hell? He swore. Hervey had better like them dead, he thought wearily.

"This one's alive," Meyers said.

The man lay alone near the rocks. He started dragging himself across the sand, groping with one outstretched hand for the gun he had dropped. He heard them. He sank down on his stomach. The sand under him turned black in the starlight. Edge knelt beside him and turned him over. He had caught a burst along the right side. The internal organs were visible in the beam of Meyers' torch. He moved his lips. Edge bent closer to hear what he was saying.

"Rain," he said. I'm getting wet inside me."

Edge had forgotten the rain. He felt it again now. They squatted beside the man and waited for him to die.

"K-Koff. I came here once when I was a boy," the man said.

"Why did you come back?" Edge asked him.

"Yeah, I could've stayed away," the man said. "But I came back. For the cause."

"What cause?"

"Koff. Go to hell," the man said. His mouth filled with blood and he died.

Edge stood up. The rain had stopped and the stars were back.

"Let's get to work," he said.

"Greene," Meyers said. "Where's Greene?"

"Tell him to come out."

Meyers spoke into his headset. "Hey, Greene. You can come out now."

The cliff threw back a soft echo. Edge swore. Why the hell had Hervey sent along such a young kid on a job like this? He swore again.

"Let's go find him," he said.

Meyers found him first. He was leaning back against a boulder staring straight ahead. There was a hole in the middle of his forehead.

"Sweet Jesus Christ," Meyers said.

"Stray bullet," Edge said. "The poor kid must've stood up to see how things were going."

"What do we do now?"

Edge took out a cell phone and made a call. "Bullfinch, this is Battle-axe."

Hervey answered immediately. "This is Bullfinch. Go ahead."

"There were five of them," Edge said.

He heard Hervey exhale slowly. "Go on," Hervey said.

"They came at us hard. They didn't leave us any choice,"

"Damn it, we needed them alive," Hervey said.

"I thought of surrounding them but it didn't work," Edge said. He took a deep breath. When he spoke again, his anger was under control. "I'm sorry," he said. "It was raining hard and it was dark as hell and there were only three of us."

"I understand," Hervey said. "I guess I'm a little jumpy. I know you did your best." He was silent for a few moments. "Did you manage to get anything from any of them?"

"Nothing. And Greene's dead."

"I'm sorry," said Hervey. "Get rid of everything, including the equipment. Put your friends in the truck and I'll have someone pick it up. Then take the boat and go to GPS reference 1105. There will be transport waiting for you. Good job and I'll see you in the morning."

Edge put away the phone and turned toward Meyers.

"We got to take the bodies to the truck," said Edge.

"Fantastic," Meyers said. "I'd like to ram my foot up Hervey's arse! That son-of-a-bitch is sitting in an air conditioned bedroom and we're out here in the blasted rain shooting at people and lugging bodies up cliffs."

Edge smiled in the darkness. "I know exactly how you feel," he said. "Gimmie a hand here."

They worked naked. The path up the cliff was steep, and they slipped often. They got the job finished eventually, then they sat down and drank a bottle of rum. Edge drew sand over the bloodstains.

"The morning tide will take care of anything we've missed," Edge said.

Meyers nodded. They stood in the surf and scrubbed themselves with sand and seawater. They pushed the boat into the water and climbed in. Meyers started the motor and set course by the Harrison Point lighthouse. Edge lay in the stern with his hands behind this head looking at the stars and seeing five men dead in the sand and Greene leaning back against a rock with a hole in the centre of his forehead.

"That's Speightstown coming up over there," Meyers said as he cut the engine.

Meyers checked his phone as Edge held onto a couple of grenades.

"Our contact has buzzed me and is on the beach waiting for us. You'll like her," said Meyers smiling.

They put their phones into waterproof plastic bags and jumped into the ocean as the boat roared away through the darkness with two grenades in the bottom. A flash lit up the water. They heard the crump of the explosion and felt the passing of the shock wave.

Edge and Meyers came onto the beach and were greeted by a woman holding some towels. Dressed in jeans and a T-shirt, she was tall with a slender waist and strong, toned legs. Her large eyes shone like stars in the moonlight.

"Good morning, gentleman," said the woman. "I was expecting a third."

"He didn't make it," said Edge, as he took one of the towels and rubbed himself dry.

"Greene was with you," she said. "He and I joined the Bureau at the same time. That's too bad. He was a good guy."

"Yes, yes. He was."

Edge pulled on some dry clothes and turned towards the car that was parked on the side of the road. The wind rustled through the palm trees as the sound of the surf rolled along behind them.

Edge leaned back in his seat and closed his eyes. His mind drifted until the car stopped. He got out and said thanks to the woman who smiled back at him. Meyers was asleep in the back seat.

Edge went straight to the shower. He came out and mixed a rum and coconut water and drank it before he left the kitchen. He took the bottle and glass into the sitting room. He stopped in front of a watercolour of a river winding through lush, green jungle. He had paid ten dollars for it in a thrift shop. Every time he looked at it, he could almost hear the voices of the canoeists coming from up river, and the sound of fish splashing in the pools downstream.

He went to the stereo and selected the jazz playlist on the MP3 player. Ella Fitzgerald's voice poured into the room like fine honey over hot cornbread. Edge poured himself another drink and sat down to wait for the dawn.

Chapter 2

The Last of the Rum

The North-east Trade winds sweep three thousand miles across the Atlantic before they hit the coconut and casuarina trees that guard the silver beaches of Barbados. Promotion brochures call the island 'paradise island' and 'island in the sun'. The English came to the island in 1625. Cotton, sugar and African slavery came a few years later. Independence followed in 1966.

Edge and Ben Jones sat in Ben's rum shop at Fustic Corner drinking and having lunch.

"Independence been around for a long time but I don't know if it change things much," Ben was saying. "Don't get me wrong, the young people getting big money, new cars and regular shopping trips to Miami, but the island still isn't theirs."

Edge took a bite out of his lunch and washed it down with ice water. The afternoon sun sent ripples of heat dancing above the asphalt road in front of the shop. A plane roared overhead. The engines changed pitch as the pilot cut his speed for the final run in to Grantley Adams International Airport.

"The old colonial shadow still falls over Barbados. The white people still own Bridgetown, the Brits and the Canadians own the banks and hotels and the economy relies on foreign investment more and more every day."

Edge looked up from his plate. "I'm not so sure what you're talking about is unique to Barbados."

"The politicians and the economists are in their pockets too," Ben said. "We have so much o' them on the island that you can't throw a rock in Bridgetown without it hitting an economist and bouncing off and cutting a politician. You know that one of them politicians even change the name o' the village he born in from Pennyhole to Gemswick? He say that 'wick' is the olde English for 'village'."

"What is he? Some kind of nut?"

Ben shrugged. He filled Edge's glass with more water and ice.

"How's tourism going?" asked Edge.

"We getting a lot o' tourists. And why not? Their dollar is worth two of ours. Rum is cheap. Sun is Free. And the beach boys are young and strong."

Edge waited.

"The beach boys here are priceless," started Ben. "They with woman all night, sleep late, pop vitamin pills and drink linseed. Some o' them so organized that they only take women who got references."

"You're kidding," Edge said.

"You don't know this thing," Ben said. "The women go back and tell their girlfriends and they come down and ask for these same boys. Sometimes them picture come down before them."

The new entreprenurial class. Edge smiled.

Ben was talking again. "The wife does put she husband on the golf course and on the deep sea fishing boat and she in the room loading. The husband does put the wife on the beach to tan and he in the room loading the maid."

"Seriously Ben," Edge asked. "How widespread is this thing?"

"I mean everybody that come down here ain't part of the package." Ben sipped his drink.

"I hear we found oil in St. Phillip," Edge said.

"Oil and gas," Ben said.

A little girl came into the shop. She ordered fifty cents in biscuits. Ben dispatched her and came and sat down again and poured another drink.

"Doctor stop me from drinking this thing," he said. "But I can't mind he."

He looked at Edge over the top of his glass. "Man you don't know how glad I is to see you," he said.

"It's good to see you too, Ben," Edge said.

There were a lot of things about the island that Edge hadn't realized he missed. Things like the laughter and the warmth of the people, and that special feeling of belonging.

"I don't feel too bad for an old man," Ben said. "Course I got to leave the women alone nowadays."

"Yeah," Edge said. "I believe you. You leave woman alone? Not you. Those grey hair might fool some people but they can't fool me."

Ben laughed. "We got a lot of drinking to catch up on. You ever went across to the continent while you were in England?"

"I went across a few times," Edge said. "It was okay."

Edge stared into the bottom of his glass of water. He had picked up the Dover-Ostend ferry one afternoon, then thumbed his way to the Mediterranean. He had planned to travel down beyond the Sahara but war stopped him in Port Said. He spent a year there before going back to England and meeting Tamora. It was months before he realized that she was an agent for the Kenyan Government. She was in London gathering intel on Sudanese rebels that were mounting attacks on Southern Sudan through Kenya. Their relationship brought Edge to the attention of the SPLA. If it wasn't for an SPLA agent pulling him out of a deadly situation with some Sudanese muscle, he may not have made it back from England.

Edge's mind drifted once more. "If it's an assassin you're looking for, you've come to the wrong man."

The High Commissioner shook his head. "No," he said. "Not that. We're setting up an Intelligence Bureau. Something quite small and compact. Responsible to the Prime Minister."

Edge studied the man behind the desk. The High Commissioner was about sixty. He had a cropped moustache, dark framed glasses and hair that was just beginning to turn grey.

Annoyance flickered briefly in the eyes behind the glasses and was gone. The smooth face was as bland as before, and the eyes held only a weary patience.

The High Commissioner raised his right hand to his temple. It was a soft, long fingered hand, with polished nails and rings on the fingers. He rubbed his fingers gently into the hair at his temple. He leaned back and closed his eyes. The hard-pressed diplomat knocking himself out in the service of his country. Edge felt almost sorry for him.

They were in the office of Franklyn Somerset, High Commissioner of Barbados to Britain, Cyprus and Australia, and Ambassador Extraordinary and Plenipotentiary to France, Sweden, Norway, Israel, Turkey and the European Community.

Somerset's eyes fluttered open. A smile flickered across his face. It wasn't a smile, really, Edge thought. It was more a sudden, fleeting change of expression that broke the wide expanse of smooth-jowled urbanity.

"Let me give it to you from the top," he said. "The Caribbean is changing fast. There's global terrorism, drugs, Mafia money, multinational corporations. There's also interest from China and the CIA. Our traditional law enforcement agencies cannot deal with those things. The Defence Force is a part-time affair. Its members shoot off blank ammunition on national holidays and go to camp once a year. That's about it. The Police have been trained to track down petty criminals and nothing more."

Somerset paused and rubbed his temple again. "Of course there's also Special Branch and the National Intelligence Committee. The Prime Minister is scrapping the Committee. All it ever does is push paper."

Somerset stared at a painting of an old Barbadian sugar-mill on the opposite wall.

"The CIA has its fingers all through the region and into South America tracking drug running, elections and political coups," he said. "We can't rely on foreigners to keep us informed anymore. It's time we looked after ourselves."

"Have you looked around the Post Office?" Edge asked.

Somerset pursed his lips. "We combed the Civil Service. We didn't have any luck."

"Who's the man in charge?"

"We brought in a man on contract," Somerset said. "Fellow named Hervey. Ex-M.I.6. Used to head the Caribbean Station of the British Secret Service at one time."

Somerset's finger traced an invisible pattern on a folder that lay on his desk.

"I know what you are thinking," he said. "But there are a couple of things. The British are no longer an imperial power, and so are unlikely to mount operations in the Caribbean. Hervey has the experience and the background to get this idea going. And he is on contract. If you take the job, you're number two until he goes."

"Somebody put you on to me," Edge said. "Who?"

Somerset tapped the folder on his desk. "It's all here," he said. "Paratroopers. London Transport. School. Your time in Kenya. Everything you've done since coming to London. Everything that matters, that is."

Well at least they got some of it right, Edge thought.

"You still haven't answered my question," he said.

Somerset lit a cigarette. He blew smoke through his nostrils and looked past Edge at a spot on the wall.

"Scotland Yard," he said. "If they had anything on you, you bet your life they would have come after you."

Edge shrugged. He didn't really care. With Tamora gone, that old restless feeling was hitting him again.

"I'll take the job," he said.

The Bureau's cover name is Sterling Industrial Consultants and the office is on Roebuck Street.

"The local CIA is our first target," Hervey was telling Edge.

Hervey was tall and thin, with a bony face, jutting nose and silver hair brushed straight back from his forehead. He wore a cream shirt and a navy-blue tie. Edge waited. Special Branch had already told them that the Political Officer at the Embassy was the CIA man on the island.

"I was thinking about the field office," Hervey said. "The man at the Embassy is chiefly liaison. They couldn't risk him in a clandestine op."

They stuck a tail on one of the known CIA agents and he led them to others, and they in turn to people higher up. After three months of possibilities they were down to four; a university professor on contract from Northwestern University, a missionary, a retired American businessman and the general manager of an American subsidiary. The computer eliminated the missionary and the retired businessman. The other two were put under long-range surveillance. Three weeks later, Edge was ready.

"Audel Firkhin, Caribbean Imports," Hervey said. "And from the look of these transcripts he is regional co-ordinator as well."

The next day, a man phoned the police and told them a bomb was planted in Minerva House. Caribbean Imports was on the second floor of Minerva House. The bomb disposal squad spent four hours inside the building.

Edge, Hervey and Audel Firkhin sat in the Conch Shell in Bridgetown.

Audel Firkhin said: "Make it quick you guys."

"I'm offering you a job," Hervey said.

"Tell me another," Firkhin said. "I like to laugh."

Firkhin had pale blue eyes and his ears stood out from his head like sails in a strong breeze.

The Bureau had taken a week to sift through the information Edge had taken from the safe in Firkhin's office.

"You're finished here," Hervey told Firkhin.

Firkhin had been reaching for his drink when Hervey spoke. He pushed the glass away. A shadow crossed his face.

"That bomb scare," he said. "That was arranged for my benefit."

Hervey ignored the comment. "They're going to love you in Washington when they hear you've been blown," he said.

Hervey studied the back of his hands. "Of course, since we are both more or less on the same side," he said. "We can dispense with the unpleasantness," He looked at Firkhin.

Hervey's accent reminded Edge of British officers in World War II films. The heir of Waterloo, fish and chips and nine hundred years of Anglo-Saxon culture hamming it up for the yokels, he thought.

"All we want is your co-operation," Hervey was saying.

Firkhin's head jerked like a stable-horse scenting smoke.

"You're out of your cotton-picking mind," he said.

"I'm not asking you to betray anybody," Hervey said quietly. "You have access to information we don't even know exists. I'm just asking you to be neighbourly. Anything you feel we ought to know, tell us. I want us to be friends, that's all."

Firkin leaned back in his chair. He tried hard to contain the relief that showed on his face.

"Anything I pass on to you guys will have to be okayed from Washington first," he said.

"Of course," Hervey said. "I quite understand that."

"Any news on Foegel?" It was Edge.

Play him gently, Hervey had said. Don't lean on him too hard. We don't want him to panic. We want him on our side, but we don't want to put him up against a wall. Foegel was a freelance gun. The intelligence services threw him the jobs that were too dirty for their own people. Between jobs, he worked part-time as an enforcer for the Mafia-king controlling the Montego Bay-Fort Lauderdale drug run. He was suspected of killing one of Firkhin's men in Antigua. The Agency had said: Get Foegel.

Firkhin had become perfectly still at the mention of Foegel's name.

"Get Foegel," Hervey said gently. "And they'll make you a general or whatever." He held Firkhin's gaze. "I'll trade him with you, but I won't give him to you for free."

The silence lasted a long time. Finally Firkhin said: "You got a deal."

"He'll be on the yacht 'Nymphette' leaving Caracas for St. Lucia Thursday next week," Hervey said. "He's yours."

"How did you find Foegel?" Edge asked. He and Hervey were walking back to the car.

"The Director of the Caribbean station of the British service is an old friend of mine," Hervey said. "Foegel used to do the odd job for him before he went bad."

"Before who went bad? Your friend or Foegel?"

"What's the matter with you?"

"You fingered Foegel, stuck him aboard a yacht and now Firkhin's waiting for him," Edge said.

Hervey shrugged. "Foegel knows the rules. A hatchet-man has no friends."

Firkhin sent Edge a bottle of bourbon whiskey a week later. Edge knew the Foegel case was closed.

He came out of a restaurant and there was a package on the seat of his car. The doors were still locked. There was no sign of forcing. He was dealing with a pro. That ruled out any possibility of a bomb. He untied the package. There was a phone inside with a note. The note read: "Graves

End. Tomorrow. 1300 hours." Firkhin hadn't bothered to sign it.

A dozen sun-and-fun fanatics from up north were toasting themselves on beach towels. A few heads bobbed in the blue-green water. The line of yachts riding at anchor beyond the breakers hardly seemed to move. Firkhin would be on one of them, he guessed – with a full supply of martinis and sun-tan lotion. He turned on the phone. It was one o'clock. The phone rang and Edge answered it.

"You're having a visitor," Firkhin said. "Bandit. Barracuda Reef." He gave Edge the date and time.

"Nothing much ever happens here," Ben's voice snapped Edge back to the present. "Nothin' much ever happens. Not like in them big countries."

"Yeah," Edge said. "It's real quiet here."

He finished his water and stood up. "Got any mauby left?" he asked Ben.

Ben reached under the counter for a glass. He filled it with mauby from a cooler in the corner.

"Best mauby this side of Canaan," he said. "Good for the heat. Cool you down real good."

"How much do I owe you?" Edge asked.

"This was my treat," Ben said. "You buy next time."

"Well, what can I say?"

"Don't say nutten, man. Come around again soon."

They shook hands and Edge went down the steps to the car.

Chapter 3

Hydrofoil Cowboy

Edge walked towards Hervey's secretary and smiled. Mabel was busy taking a call, but she returned his smile and motioned for him to proceed into Hervey's office.

Hervey's face was grey. The lines seemed deeper. He passed his hand through his hair.

"Morning Shannon," he said. "I don't suppose you got any sleep either. Look, I'm sorry I screamed at you last night."

"Don't worry about it," Edge said.

"The bodies were buried at sea a few hours ago," Hervey said. "And I just handed my report to the Prime Minister about half an hour ago."

"Greene. What about him?"

"Covered," Hervey said. "And the cover story has been introduced into the pipeline."

Edge didn't ask what the cover story was. That was Hervey's headache.

"Did we find out the names of the five men?"

Hervey shook his head. "Special Branch is still working on it."

One of the phones on the desk rang. Hervey picked it up. He said "Hello" into the mouthpiece then sat listening without saying anything. Finally he said: "I'll send him over."

He put the phone down. "That was Special Branch," he said. "Assistant Commissioner Cooper. He thinks he might have something for us."

"That was quick," Edge said. He didn't think Cooper would've been that quick.

"It's not about the five men," Hervey said. "The Assistant Commissioner wants to talk to you about something else."

Edge drove slowly through the late morning traffic. Driving in the city was easy on the eyes. Skirts had gone up a few years ago and had stayed up. Some of the legs were exceptional. The women had an easy, flowing unselfconscious rhythm and enormous vitality. Edge had seen any number of beautiful women, but he had never seen them so thick on the ground as in the Caribbean. A woman in a form fitting green and beige dress stepped on to the pedestrian crossing and flashed him a smile. His eyes stayed with her until she reached the other side.

Cooper said: "Glad you could come."

He was a slim man, with alert confident eyes. He looked hard and durable, as though the sun and the rain and other people's troubles had brought out some hidden strength in him.

"Hervey said you had something for us."

Cooper took a bunch of keys. They went down the corridor past a row of offices and came to the cells. Cooper unlocked one at the end of the row. Edge followed him inside. A man lay on the bunk against the wall. Grey stubble showed through the sagging flesh on his face. His clothes were dirty and he smelled of stale sweat and alcohol. He sat up slowly and blinked at the two men through watery eyes.

"I need a drink," he said. "I need a drink bad."

Cooper said: "I brought a drink for you."

He took a flask of rum from his hip pocket. He snapped the cork and passed the bottle to the man on the bunk. Boozy wiped the inside of his mouth with his tongue. He closed his eyes, held his head back and poured a mouthful of rum. The drink shook him. He held onto the bunk and waited until the shuddering stopped. He passed his hand over his face and wiped away the rum that trickled down his chin.

"Lets hear that story of yours again, Boozy," Cooper said gently.

Boozy glanced from Edge to Cooper and back.

"He's a friend of mine," Cooper said. "I want you to tell him what you told me."

"There's going to be a big bank robbery," Boozy said slowly.

Edge looked at Cooper. Cooper's face showed nothing at all.

"The banks on Broad Street," Boozy went on. He counted them on his fingers. "On Independence morning. While everyone is watching the parade. They're bringing men from outside."

Edge came off the wall. Boozy grinned at him slyly.

"How does he know about this?" he asked.

"I know," said Boozy. "I heard men talking."

"Who's going to hit the Broad Street banks?" Edge asked.

"I didn't see them," Boozy said. "It was dark. I was sleeping on a bench in the park and I hear voices. But it was too dark. They was talking about the robbery." He raised the bottle to his lips again.

"Maybe you were dreaming, Boozy," Edge said.

Boozy shook his head. "No. I hear them. But it too dark for me to see."

"Did they know you were there?"

"I dunno. I got frighten' and I run. I don't know if them see me. He lay back against the wall. His eyes measured the amount of rum left in the bottle. Cooper followed Edge out.

"Send for me when you are ready," Cooper said. They left him clutching the flask of rum to his bosom.

"Is your man Boozy reliable?"

"He has given us a few good things over the years and no matter what I do I can't shake him from this story."

Cooper went and sat down behind his desk. Edge leaned against the wall.

"Independence anniversary," Edge said. "We've got four days."

Cooper said: "I've got every available man working on those identities for you." He went to the tap and caught water in a kettle and came back and plugged it in.

"The morning of the big parade," Edge said. "A national holiday. Bridgetown deserted. The regiment and the police will be at the Savannah entertaining the crowd. Half a dozen good men could swing it."

"And get away with it," Cooper added.

The kettle started humming. Cooper pulled the plug.

"Motive?" He spooned coffee into two cups and added water.

"Black," Edge said.

Cooper passed a cup to Edge and added milk and sugar for himself.

"The obvious one is money," Edge said. "There's a lot of it in those banks."

"There's something else." Cooper put down his cup and looked at Edge.

"Okay there's the political angle," Edge said. "Hit those banks and the economy collapses. Nobody gets paid. Even the civil servants will take to the streets. The whole nation will be marching. Marching for food. You can guess the rest."

"Yeah," Cooper said. "Riots, then a revolution. Every major act has political consequences whether those consequences are intended or not."

"Let's suppose they're just bandits," Edge said. "How would they get away?" He knew the answer before Cooper answered.

"Sea," Cooper said. "We can't watch every cove and bay twenty-four hours a day."

Edge put his cup down on a table. "Given the national passion for mediocrity," he said. "I don't see how a local group could possibly be behind this.

"I'm with you," Cooper said. He reached for his hat. "Let's go see a yacht."

"Yours?"

"Yeah, mine," Cooper said. He locked the drawers of his desk and they went out. "Went to the supermarket lately and seen those fancy prices?" he asked Edge. "I used to drink scotch once in a while. I'm back to rum permanently now. And I could use a new car, but I can't even finish paying for the old one yet."

Cooper's car was an old Toyota. He unlocked for Edge, then got in.

"This yacht is called the 'Liberty Queen'. Out of Galveston, Texas. Got in yesterday morning. Owned by one Thomas Bunker Hill. There are a few other freighters in port but none of them arrived after this yacht. I've got men checking out those too."

The 'Liberty Queen' was riding at anchor about a hundred yards from the shore. Edge and Cooper stepped aboard a police cutter that was waiting for them. The cutter ran up alongside the 'Liberty Queen'. A man appeared on the deck above them.

"Police," Cooper called. "We're coming aboard."

The man caught the rope Cooper threw to him. They climbed aboard.

"Thomas Bunker Hill," the man said. He held out his hand. "What can I do for you?"

Cooper showed him his card. Hill looked at it and passed it back. Hill was about six foot six and the cigar in his mouth looked only fractionally shorter. He was about seventy. His hair was white and there was a network of fine lines across his craggy face. The eyes reminded Edge of pebbles at the bottom of a pool. He wore a dark blue shirt open at the throat, grey slacks and cowboy boots. Edge looked around for the white Stetson, but he did not see it.

"Could I see your papers?" Cooper asked. "And the passports."

A voice behind Edge said: "Is there a problem Mister Hill? If so, I'll gladly dump the trash overboard for you."

Edge turned. The man came off the rails and stood facing him. He wore a red and blue polo shirt, beige pants and heavy, oil-blackened boots. The arms were thick and covered in coarse, black hair. Part of one ear was missing. He topped Edge by at least four inches and by about thirty pounds. He looked fast on his feet and very sure of himself.

"Is that any way to welcome guests on your boss's boat?" Edge asked politely.

"I have my welcome mat right here," he said.

The man's smile disappeared. The eyes narrowed and the left shoulder dropped. Edge stepped inside the right hook and hit him in the stomach. It was like hitting a tree. The man blinked and stepped back. There was a look of surprise on his face. Edge guessed that right hook had won him a lot of fights. The man's hand dipped into his pocket and came up with a set of brass knuckles. Edge moved back. The sun glinted on the brass knuckles. Edge dropped to the deck and kicked the man's left ankle from under him. He came up outside the blur of the brass knuckles and drove the heel of his left hand under the man's chin, snapping the head back on the powerful neck. Edge tapped him in the throat with the side of his hand and cracked him on the point of his jaw with his elbow. The man sat down and blinked his eyes hard. Edge helped him to his feet. He had difficulty staying upright.

"You owe me an apology," Edge said.

The man held his fingers against his jaw and opened and closed his mouth a few times. He looked at Edge. There was something in his eyes that was not there before.

"I didn't mean no offence," he said.

"No hard feelings," Edge said.

Edge walked across the deck to where Cooper and Hill waited. Cooper's face wore a look of weary disapproval as Hill studied him from behind a bleak smile.

"I can't imagine what got into my man Trask," Hill said. "He's usually very quiet and reliable. I trust you gentlemen will overlook the incident."

"There's probably a heart of gold under that rough exterior," Edge said.

The eyes continued to study him.

The yacht's papers showed Hill had sailed from Galveston five weeks earlier, and had stopped at Nassau and Jamaica on his way to Barbados. He told them he'd always wanted to sail the Caribbean but that he'd never got the chance until then. He told them he was mixing business with pleasure, that he was keeping an eye out for investment opportunities.

"Anything wrong?" he asked, as Cooper passed the papers back to him.

Cooper told him everything was fine.

"Was that really necessary?" Cooper asked Edge as they stepped onto the pier.

"Yes," Edge answered.

"If you take on everybody who thinks like Trask," Cooper said. "You're going to have a lot of trouble on your hands."

"There're worse kinds of trouble," Edge said.

Cooper opened his mouth to say something, changed his mind and gave himself a cigarette instead. He parked the car and told Edge he would have the names ready in a couple of days. Edge said he would tell Hervey.

"Does Cooper believe this Boozy?" Hervey asked.

"Difficult to tell," Edge said. "Cooper doesn't give away much."

"All right," Hervey said. "So you think the story's a plant."

"It's just a feeling I got," Edge said.

"What about Hill?"

"Cruising the Caribbean looking for investment opportunities," Edge said. "Owns a yacht and a few millions. Made his money in oil by the sound of things. Knows all the right people both here and in the U.S. Any minute now, somebody is going to elect him Chairman of the Barbadian League of Coconut Pickers."

Nothing showed on Hervey's face.

"Audel Firkhin flew out of Barbados yesterday morning," he said matter-of-factly.

"Lucky son-of-a-gun," Edge said.

His head ached. There was grit behind the eyelids. His mouth tasted of the previous night's rum, of powder smoke and fresh blood. Perhaps it would help if I went to the washroom and made myself sick, he thought. But he knew he wouldn't go. He leaned back in his chair and tuned out Hervey's voice. The sun streamed in through the open window. From where he sat, he could see the tops of trees shining bright-green in the sun. A sparrow flew on to the window-sill, cocked an inquisitive eye at the two men, hopped a few steps, decided there were no crumbs to be had and flew off. On the street below, a woman with a tray of vegetables on her head passed singing a calypso.

"The Minister of Technology, Planning and Development wants to see you in his office at eleven."

Hervey's voice seemed to come from a long way off, from another world almost.

Chapter 4

Coffee Break

Edge parked the car beside the silver Audi and went up the stairs to the Ministry of Technology, Planning and Development. The building was an old plantation house outside the city. Almanacs, photographs of Cabinet ministers, and the Barbados coat-of-arms looked down from walls where family portraits had hung for centuries.

The receptionist looked up from her computer. "May I help you?" she said.

"The name is Edge. I'm here to see the Minister."

"Oh, yes. He's engaged at the moment, but I don't think he'll be long. He's expecting you."

He smiled at her. The smile she gave him in return was full of surprise and wariness. He wondered when last a man had smiled at her. Must've been a long time ago when she was young, before the lines of bitterness and mistrust had begun to furrow her brow and etch that hardness around the corners of her mouth, he thought.

"That's a real nice perfume you're wearing," he said.

"You're very kind."

"I'll wait out here until the Minister is free," Edge said.

"No, come inside," she said. She opened the door and showed him to a seat near her desk. Half a dozen heads lifted briefly, then the 'clack-clack' of keyboards resumed as fingers took up their march across their keys.

A door on the far side of the room opened. The Minister and Thomas Bunker Hill came out. Hill had a white Stetson in one hand and a cigar in the other. His eyes swept past Edge then came back. His face lit up and he came over to Edge with his hand extended.

"Mr. Edge," he said. "I just called your name a moment ago."

Edge said, "Hello." They shook hands.

"Good to see you," Hill said. "Good to see you."

The receptionist opened the door for Hill, and he went out.

The Hon. Mervin Steele said: "Shannon Edge. How long has it been?"

"Almost ten years," Edge said.

They went into Steele's office.

"Good to see you again," Steele said. "I heard you were in Europe and then Africa doing all sorts of interesting and exciting things."

Steele hadn't changed much. He was a small man. Remembering him from school-days, Edge had expected him to be bigger. The face was sharp and thin. There were hardly any lips. The eyes that used to terrify the junior forms when Steele was Head Prefect now gazed at Edge with frank and friendly interest. Edge glanced around the room.

"Congratulations," he said.

Steele shrugged. "I was lucky," he said. "I managed to get through a couple of universities overseas, and when I came back, I was invited to sit in the Senate. I managed to win a seat last elections. That's about all."

"Married?"

"Too busy. What about you? Heard you were in the army."

Edge shrugged. "A youthful indiscretion you might say. But I caught myself in time. Managed to do a few of the things I've always wanted to do."

"The High Commissioner sent us a report," Steele said. "I'm glad you decided to take the job."

The office was air-conditioned and panelled in cedar and mahogany. The carpet was deep and soft and new. Steele drew a folder towards him.

"The Prime Minister asked me to handle this matter for him," he said. "I've seen Hervey's report, but I want to hear from you."

Edge told him what he knew.

"This character, what do you think of his story?"

"We can't afford to dismiss him."

Steele took off his glasses, wiped them and put them on again. "With this economy and the global threat of terror we can't take any more shocks at the moment. If those banks get hit we're in for serious trouble." He smiled suddenly. "Sorry, but I've got to think of this like a politician. There're tourists and investors to think about. Whatever else happens we must keep them coming." He shook his head. "We're lucky you intercepted those men on the beach last night. I would hate to know they were roaming loose on the island."

Edge didn't say anything. He waited for Steele to go on.

"The Prime Minister said to tell you thanks," Steele said. "You're to carry out your investigations as vigorously as possible, but on no account must the public get wind of what's going on." The Minister raised his eyes to the ceiling. "What are we coming to? A few years ago anything like this would have been unthinkable."

"Like the man said, change is the only constant," Edge offered.

"Yes, but why only for the worst?" Steele said. "There seems to be a dangerous element loose in this country" The eyes behind the steel-rimmed glasses flickered briefly. "Do you carry a gun?"

"Sometimes."

"Naturally, I don't want you taking any unnecessary risks," Steele said. "But I'd like to see you keep the gun-play to a minimum while you are following this thing up."

"I know," Edge said. "Guns scare off tourists and investors."

"No need to get angry," the Minister said. "The rest is routine anyhow, and even if those five men have friends here they won't dare make a move now that they know we killed the men that were coming to help them. And another thing, I'd like a daily report. I hope that's not asking too much."

A knock sounded at the door. Steele said come in. The door opened and the receptionist came in with two cups of coffee on a tray.

"I hope you like coffee," Steele said.

Edge took his black without sugar. Steele had his with milk and sugar.

"Thank you Miss Chanson," Steele said. Miss Chanson smiled shyly. She went out, closing the door behind her.

"I heard you met Mr. Thomas Bunker Hill," Steele said.

"Yes, and his man Gila Trask."

"Hill phoned the American Ambassador demanding an apology."

"And did he get his apology?"

The Prime Minister got in touch with me, and called Assistant Commissioner Cooper. The Ambassador apologized." Steele put down his cup. "Thomas Bunker Hill is thinking about putting some money into that new refinery we're building. Nothing settled yet, but I think he means business."

Edge finished his coffee. The Minister stood up.

"You must call me up some Sunday morning. Let's have a round of golf," Steele said.

"Cricket is all I can manage," Edge said. "Saves caddy's fees."

Steele laughed. "We must get together again," he said.

Edge said yes. They shook hands.

The lunch hour rush caught him on the way back and added fifteen minutes to what was normally a ten-minute ride.

"The Prime Minister was on the phone," Hervey said. "The Bureau is to report to Steele."

"The Prime Minister must think very highly of Steele," said Edge.

"So I've heard," Hervey said.

"Steele said no guns. Didn't want to frighten the tourists."

"The Prime Minister said the same thing."

"We also have to give Steele a daily report," Edge said.

"That's the trouble with these armchair strategists," Hervey said. "They're a pain in the ass."

They had lunch at the "Feeding Trough", a new restaurant overlooking the harbour. A waitress in a short red skirt and a white blouse led them to a seat near one of the windows. The place was nearly full. Pieces of African sculpture hung from the walls and ceiling. Potted plants stood in the corners. Music came from the speakers set in the walls and ceiling. Edge ordered dolphin in white sauce, green bananas and pigeon peas. Hervey ordered fish and chips.

"This place is becoming popular," Hervey said.

"It has a lot going for it," Edge said. "Good food, atmosphere and women that are easy on the eyes."

The waitress cleared the table.

"Cooper identified one of the men," Hervey said. "Name is Boris White. Used to live with an uncle in some village called Taitt Hill. I understand that his uncle thinks of himself as some sort of High Priest. He is the leader of a cult called 'The Remnant of Judah'."

"At least we have some place to start."

"There is something else," Hervey said.

Edge waited.

"The police fished Boozy's body out of the careenage this afternoon," Hervey said. "Cooper thought that you would like to know."

Poor devil, Edge thought. He wondered who would want Boozy dead.

Hervey looked at Edge and said quietly: "There are no coincidences in this business."

Chapter 5

The Prophet

Edge drove slowly through the hot afternoon with the breeze blowing in off the sea, and the sun bringing little silver flashes leaping from the water. He saw the sign marked 'Taitt Hill' and he swung into the narrow road between two rows of houses. The sign merely meant that Taitt Hill was in that general direction. Edge drew near a sandbox tree where a group of men sat playing dominoes. He stuck his head out of the window. One of the men put the cards face down on the table and came over to him. Edge asked him where Taitt Hill was. The man pointed down the road and told Edge to turn left, then right then left again, and he would see Taitt Hill in front of him.

Edge said thanks and slid the car into gear. A few minutes later a little boy with a bucket of water on his head pointed to a cluster of wooden houses on a hill and told him that was Taitt Hill.

Edge parked the car and left the windows down and followed the rocky path that wound through a gully and up the hill. Edge felt the perspiration gather between his shoulders and course down inside his shirt. He stopped near an unpainted wooden building with narrow oblong windows and a cross on the roof. Edge knocked on the house beside the church. Nobody answered. He knocked again. A man came around the corner of the house.

"Was't thou knocking long?" the man asked. "I was in the temple and did not hear thee."

The man was old, near seventy. He wore a full-length black robe belted around his middle with a piece of rope. He was bare-footed. His hair was long and tangled and hung like an off-white mop above his charcoal face. His beard, matted like his hair, reached almost to his waist. The eyes that stared back at Edge were calm and untroubled.

"Mr. White?"

"Yes, I'm Josh White."

"My name's Edge. I'd like to speak to you for a few minutes."

"Come with me into the orchard," White said. "It's cooler there."

They sat on a makeshift bench nailed to a cherry tree.

"It's about my nephew," White said. "No?"

Edge said: "Yes. How did you guess?"

White sighed. "I is an old man," he said. "Nobody coming all the way up here to see me. My nephew now, he young and full of foolishness of youth. If strangers come, is him they seek."

"Boris left Barbados some time ago. Do you know where he went or who sent him?"

"Ah, a policeman," White said. "I knew as soon as I see you. Why do you want to know these things?"

"I am sort of a policeman," Edge said. "Do you know anything about where Boris went?"

White reached up with one hand and picked a handful of cherries and held them out to Edge.

"If I had my way," White said. "I'd plant rows of cherry trees at the side of the highway. I can see them now in August, red and green and yellow and the birds eating them, and the little children under the trees with their paper bags picking up those that fall."

Edge chewed a couple of cherries and spat out the seeds and waited.

"All Boris told me was that he was going to New York," White said. "I asked him where he got the money, but he never say."

"Any messages, e-mails or letters?"

White shook his head. "But it doesn't matter no more, the boy is dead."

"Who told you that?"

White put his hand over his heart. "I know it here," he said. He looked away into the distance. "The boy came to me in the night while I was in the temple. There was blood on his shirt and he was afraid."

"A dream," Edge said. "People get them sometimes."

"Not so," White said. "I know."

"Who are his friends? Did he bring any of them home?"

"No," White said. "I think he was ashamed of his old uncle. I took him when his mother died. I fed him and I gave him clothes. He became my son, but in the end he is ashamed."

"Tell me about yourself," Edge said.

"There is nothing to tell." White said. For the first time there was a tinge of anger in his voice. "In a land where every man wears a price-tag, I is my own man. I loves the land, and it gives me enough to feed myself. When I not in the land, I in the temple." He studied Edge's face. "I trying to lead my people back to God," he said quietly.

The orchard was still except for the song of birds. Edge leaned against the trunk of the cherry tree and watched the branches move against the sky.

"That's strange," White said. "You didn't laugh."

"I didn't think it was funny," Edge said.

"I started my church twenty-three years ago," White said. "We are a small group. The Remnant of Judah. We'll always be remnant. We don't offer no creeds or dogmas, only prayer and contemplation. We read the Book through once a year, and on Saturdays, we sit down to a ceremonial meal of biscuits and lemonade."

"You don't believe in bread and wine then?"

"Jesus the Brother used what he had," White said. "We does the same."

"And Boris," Edge said. "He ever came?"

"Once when he is very young. Then he followed the daughters of Midian."

"Who?"

"Women who paints their faces and expose themselves to the eyes of men," White said.

"Look," Edge said. "I'm trying to find out about your nephew. I need your help."

"Boris never worked. He formed part of the twenty-seven per cent. As for his friends, I never met them."

Edge stood up. "Well, thanks anyway," he said.

White stood up slowly. "Your job is dangerous," he said. "Do you enjoy your work?"

"It's just a job," Edge said. "A tough, difficult job that nobody wants."

"Each of us does what he must do," White said.

"Yes, I suppose so."

White walked with him across the yard and around to the front of the house.

"I'm sorry about the boy," Edge said.

"He was all I had left," White said softly. "Still, the Lord giveth, and the Lord taketh away. Blessed be the name of the Lord."

Edge rested his hand on the man's shoulder. "I'm sorry," he said again.

White turned to face Edge. The look of pain on his face made Edge wince, then the mask dropped into place and the old man's face was serene again.

"Have you ever heard of the Columbus Club?"

Edge said no, he didn't.

"Find out what you can about it," White said.

Edge went home. He showered and changed and drove to the cemetery. The mourners stood around Greene's coffin singing 'They Have Come From Tribulation, And Have Washed Their Robes In Blood'. He saw Hervey's secretary, Mabel Hillier put her wreath down on the coffin and go up to a tall middle-aged woman who was crying into a handkerchief. Edge went to the woman and shook her hand and told her that he was sorry. She looked at him and nodded and he knew she wasn't seeing him, and that the pain and shock had cut deep, and that she didn't even have tears left.

Edge got the address of the Columbus Club from Cooper. He used the fire escape at the back of the building to get to the third floor where Cooper told him the office was. The second key he tried worked. He pushed the door open and went inside. He flashed his torch around and drew the curtains closer and switched on the light. He saw a filing cabinet and two desks. The dust on them looked six inches deep. The clock on the Public Building's tower struck two.

The noise was so slight that it could have been the curtains rustling in the breeze. Edge threw himself to one side. Something brushed his shoulder and drew a shower of sparks from the edge of the filling cabinet. Edge turned. The man wore a stocking over his face. He had a two-foot piece of iron pipe in his hand. The man lunged and swung the iron pipe at Edge. The pipe smashed against the desk as Edge ducked out of the way. The man swung wildly behind him as Edge leaned backwards to evade the attack. Dropping the flashlight, Edge picked up a chair. He threw it. One of the legs hit the man on the chin. The iron pipe went flying behind the man. He fell to one knee. Edge waited. The man came up off the floor. Part of the stocking was ripped away and one ear stuck out through the rent. The man charged at Edge and slammed him into a wall. Edge's head snapped to the side as the man connected with a right hook. Edge slapped the man around his ears causing him to stagger back. A kick to the chest sent the man to the ground once again. Edge picked up the chair as the man came up on his knees. While on the ground the man glanced over his shoulder at the door to the fire escape. The man scrambled to his feet and Edge let him reach the door.

The man opened the door and Edge heard him running down the fire escape.

Edge looked around the room. Somebody had already cleaned it out. He wasn't surprised now that he knew they had been expecting him. The man hadn't really wanted to kill him. Somebody decided that putting him in hospital was enough – for the time being at least. He turned off the light and went down the fire escape. Edge used his cell phone to call Hervey. He sounded half asleep.

"Sorry to get you out of bed," Edge said.

"Fine, fine. You've had your laugh. Now what's the story?"

"I just left the Columbus Club. Nothing there. They moved out a long time ago. Get Cooper to run a check on old man White."

"Very well."

"That's about it for now," Edge said.

"Forget about your reports," said Hervey. "I'll look after them for you. One other thing. It was hard to find, but intel was able to come up with something about the Club from few years ago. It's a name: Charles Hardcastle."

Edge told Hervey thanks. He went home and gave himself a couple of rums and coconut water and went to bed.

Chapter 6

Body Heat

The house was on the crest of a low rise looking south towards the sea - a low ranch-style building done in white coral tone. Vine clustered thick on the pillars of the verandah. Bright yellow flowers peeped between the leaves. Gardens followed the contours of the ground east and south of the house. A tennis court was west of the house and an orchard was on the other side. A border of soft green grass separated the landscaped gardens from the bougainvillea hedge. The top of the hedge was covered with small red flowers.

Edge pressed the doorbell and waited. The door opened. She had been in the bath. One hand held the robe close at her throat. The other brushed back her wet hair. She smelled fresh and clean like the earth after a late morning shower of rain.

She had red hair and grey eyes and there was a sprinkling of freckles under the tan of her cheeks.

"My name is Shannon Edge," he said. "I want to talk to Charles."

"Come in," she said. The voice was low and cool. "I'm his sister, Shelley. Perhaps I can help you."

She moved aside and Edge stepped past her.

"Give me a minute," she said. "This is the servants' day off and things are a bit unsettled. Make yourself comfortable while I get into some clothes." She indicated a chair and left him.

The chair was softer and deeper than it looked and he made a grab at the table near him before he finally came to rest less than six inches from the floor.

He took up an old photograph from the table. It showed a middle-aged couple with two small children. There were a number of photographs of a man Edge guessed was Charles, mostly on yachts and gazing at the sea. There were a few of Shelley riding horses, playing tennis and lying on the beach.

Special Branch had given him some background on the Hardcastles. They owned a plantation somewhere in the country. Charles Hardcastle sailed yachts and played polo. Shelley had been to school in England, had married an Englishman, divorced him and returned home. Both parents were dead.

He heard Shelly come into the room. She wore a loose fitting blouse and a pair of pants. She had brushed her hair and tied it with a green band. She wasn't wearing a bra. She sat down opposite him and crossed her legs. She took a cigarette from the box at her elbow. Edge leaned across and snapped the lighter under her cigarette and put the lighter back beside the lacquered coconut shell ashtray with the calypso dancers on it.

Shelley settled back into her chair. "You said you wanted to see my brother," she began.

She leaned her head back and looked at him from behind lowered lids. She swung her left arm across her body just below her breasts and gripped the elbow of the hand holding the cigarette.

"I don't think you can help me, Miss Hardcastle," Edge said.

"Try me," she answered. "And call me Shelley."

"I'm from the Currency Control Division," Edge said.

"Got anything that says so?"

Edge took a card from his wallet and handed it to her. She looked at it and handed it back to him.

"Charles has gone on a fishing trip," she said. "It'll be at least a couple of days before he gets back."

"Ever heard of the Columbus Club?" He asked the question casually and he saw her start. She dragged hard on the cigarette and blew a cloud of smoke at the open window.

"No," she said. "Never."

"Charles used to be secretary," Edge said.

"I never heard him say anything about it," she said. She sat up suddenly. "Damn," she said. "I forgot to turn off the heater."

Edge watched her leave the room. She had very nice legs. He closed his eyes and waited. He heard her come back. He opened his eyes. She had a gun.

"Get out of this house," she said. "Now, before this thing goes off and punches little holes in you."

Edge stood up. "Guns never solve anything," he said quietly.

He started towards her. The gun remained pointing at his navel. He kept his eyes in hers. He reached out and took the gun from her.

"It was empty anyway," she said, and sat down. "Okay, you called my bluff, but I also called yours. Currency Control Division? Hardly. You've faced guns before."

"I'm not a policeman, if that's what you mean," he said.

"I need something to drink. What's yours?" she asked as she walked towards the liquor cabinet.

Edge told her. She came back pushing a portable bar.

"You're lucky," she said. "I got some coconuts cut only yesterday."

She put ice in the glass, then added rum and coconut water. She took scotch and soda.

"Cheers," she said. They raised glasses.

"Charles is in trouble isn't he? Something to do with this...this..." She searched for the name, found it. "This Columbus Club."

"He's not in any trouble," Edge said. "I just want him to tell me what he knows."

"Let me freshen yours," she said.

He held the glass out to her. Their fingers touched. She put both glasses down on the bar. Edge got up and she came back and gave him his drink. Their fingers touched again and she smiled.

"Charles got a call early yesterday morning," she said. "I answered the phone but didn't recognize the voice. Charles left immediately on the fishing trip."

Edge finished his drink and walked out onto the verandah. He thanked her and gave her the number to the Bureau's answering service.

"If he calls you, get in touch with me at this number."

He got into his car and drove away from the house as Shelley stood in the verandah.

Mabel Hiller was doing the crossword when he walked in.

"Ah, you can help me here," she said. "'Song heard in the procession of the sad and perceptive'. Four letters."

"Watch it with the four letter words Mabel," he said.

"Okay, so you don't know."

"Try 'keen'," he said.

"Miss Hillier, I thought I told you to let me know as soon as Shannon came in." It was Hervey. Edge hadn't heard him come into the outer office.

Mabel folded the paper and put it away. "Mr. Edge, Mr. Hervey wants to see you right away."

Hervey sat behind his desk facing Edge. "Cooper says there was someone waiting for you at the Columbus Club."

"It was nothing much," Edge said. "He wanted to scare me. He got away and I didn't get a good look at his face."

"You didn't think it important enough to tell me about it?" Hervey said.

Edge let the question pass. "Did Special Branch get a lead on him?" he asked.

Hervey said no, that there were no fingerprints. Edge shrugged.

"Cooper had old man White checked out," Hervey said. "He hasn't left that village for as long as anybody can remember."

Edge told him about Charles Hardcastle and the early morning call. Hervey nodded. Edge knew that he had already decided to put Shelley under surveillance.

"Oh, another thing," Hervey said almost as an after thought. "Special Branch came up with a few more names."

He took a sheet of paper from his desk and handed it to Edge. "All locals it seems. I've sent you the file."

Edge glanced through the names on the printout. He gave the sheet back to Hervey.

"The Minister phoned," Hervey said. "Wanted to know what progress we had made."

"Did he have any suggestions?" Edge asked.

"He spoke words of encouragement," Hervey said.

Edge stood up. He told Hervey he was going home. He was tired. The names on the list could wait until the next day.

Chapter 7

Flash Point

Edge opened his eyes and stared at the ceiling. He had been dreaming about Shelley Hardcastle. He could not remember the details. He got out of bed and went to the window. He opened the window and stood with his arms extended and took twelve deep, slow breaths. He turned away from the window and lay down on the floor and hooked his toes under the dresser and did sit-ups until his stomach muscles screamed.

He got up and went to the bathroom. He came back, took an egg from the refrigerator and dropped it into a saucepan of water. He heard the newspaper hit against the door and he pulled on a pair of pants and opened the door and picked up the paper. He took the egg out of the saucepan and got a bottle of beer from the refrigerator and sat down and opened the paper.

He heard a knock on the door.

"It's open," he said.

The door opened and a voice said: "Morning Mr. Edge."

Edge said: "Morning Wenceslas."

Wenceslas Rowley was 12 years old. Twice a week, he came to clean Edge's car. The last time he came, he had won a dollar a week raise from Edge. He stood in the doorway now waiting for the keys.

"I bet you I win this time," he said.

"Bet you not," said Edge.

"I'll win," said Wenceslas. "And if I do, you owe me another raise."

Edge let the paper fall. He scooped the keys off the table and whirled and flicked them to the boy's left. Wenceslas' hand shot out. He raised his hand and his smile was like a star-burst.

"I see you looking to my left," he said.

"You're going to put me in the poorhouse," said Edge.

Edge and Wenceslas walked out of the house and onto the driveway where Edge's car was parked next to a soapy bucket and some sponges.

"If the West Indies had you in the team we would've beaten Australia. Let me know when you're done," Edge said. "We'll take some lunch to your sister."

Edge turned and walked back to the house as Wenceslas got into the driver's seat. The earth shook suddenly. The force of the explosion lifted Edge off of his feet and sent him flying into the air. Edge rolled onto his stomach and blinked several times to clear his blurred vision. The ringing in his ears made his head ache even worse. Part of the car was beside him near the front steps. Another piece was in the driveway. The rest blazed near the garage door. Wenceslas Rowley was hunched forward over the wheel wrapped in flames.

Edge stumbled to his feet and started towards the car. "Oh my God," he breathed.

Hands held him back. He tried to break free. He heard himself swearing. Through the ringing in his ears a voice kept repeating, "There is nothing you can do." He shook his head and suddenly he was as calm as the eye of a hurricane.

A siren sounded in the distance. A fire engine swung into the street. An ambulance followed. The firemen turned their hoses on the flames and they hissed and popped and died.

After being looked at by the paramedics, Edge went into the house. He poured a double rum and drank it neat. He called Hervey. Two uniformed attendants placed the body in a blanket and lifted it into the ambulance. He heard the ambulance drive away.

"You must've scared someone to no end to make them try a thing like that," Hervey was saying.

Edge didn't say anything. He was thinking about the boy.

"It wasn't your fault," Hervey said. "Don't take it so hard. Give me the boy's address and we'll notify his family."

Edge gave him Wenceslas' sister's address.

"Send someone to pick up the wreckage while you're at it," he said.

"Don't worry," Hervey said. "I'll look after the arrangements."

Edge put down the phone. His hands were still shaking. He had another drink and then wrote a note for the cleaning lady and left it on the table. He called a taxi and drove to Saul's garage.

"How you been?" Saul greeted him.

Saul was ex-Special Branch. One day a machete-wielding suspect chopped off his right arm and Saul took his gratuity and went into business for himself. Ten of the cars in the fleet were on permanent standby for the Bureau.

"I need one of your cars," Edge said.

"You had an accident?"

Saul had a paunch. The empty sleeve flapped whenever he moved. The memory of something terrible lurked in the shadows behind his eyes.

"Ignition bomb," Edge said.

Saul looked away. He had troubles of his own. The machete had taken more than his right arm. He still awoke sometimes at night sweating, haunted by the memory of a part of himself lying at his feet.

"What about a Volkswagen," Saul said. "I had it tuned yesterday."

"The Volks will be fine," Edge said.

"Did you say a bomb?" Saul asked Edge. "How did you escape?"

"It killed a little boy," Edge said. "He started the car and the bomb went off."

"Take care," Saul said. "They'll try for you again."

"Don't worry, we'll get the car back to you," Edge said.

"I'm not worried about the car," Saul said.

The house was a two-bedroom cottage behind a hedge of sweet lime. He knocked and Fenella Rowley opened for him.

"Good morning Miss Rowley. My name is Edge. I'm sorry about your brother."

She said: "Come in."

She was a big, soft woman, with calm, intelligent eyes.

"I came to say that I'm sorry," Edge said. "I don't know what to say. Wenceslas died in my place."

"It's not your fault," she said. "Wenceslas just happened to be in the wrong place at the wrong time."

"I'm really very sorry," he said again. He couldn't remember ever feeling so helpless before.

"Wenceslas was always talking about you," Fenella said. "I think you were a combination of father and big brother in his eyes."

Edge shook his head. He hadn't known this.

"Our mother died when he was three," Fenella said. She didn't say anything about his father.

"Is there anything I can do?" Edge asked.

Too late, he thought. Much too late; like so many things in human experience.

"A man called," Fenella said. "Said he'd be sending someone around."

Hervey, Edge thought.

"His birthday is tomorrow," Fenella said. "I baked the cake early."

The tears started. Fenella dabbed her eyes with a handkerchief. The tears came faster.

Edge put his arm around her. He let her cry. She lifted her chin and looked at him and he gave her his handkerchief and she dropped her wet one on the chair and wiped her eyes with slow, deliberate movements.

"I promised myself that I wouldn't do this," she said.

She handed him the handkerchief, and he looked into her eyes and saw their compassion and strength and courage, and he said: "I'm sorry we had to meet like this." He opened the door and let himself out.

Danny Powson's name was at the top of the list. He lived in East Parade. East Parade was an old money area. Years ago people who were caught walking through there risked arrest unless they could prove to the satisfaction of the police that they were domestics or 'gardener boys'.

The name of the house was 'Wessex'. Edge parked and pushed open a large iron gate. The driveway was a closed zipper on a patchwork quilt of roses, violets, marigolds, lilies and carnations. An old woman was kneeling in the garden. She wore yellow gloves and had a pair of shears in her hand.

"The servant's entrance is around the back." She said it without looking up.

"Thanks," said Edge. "I'll keep that in mind."

She straightened up and looked at him. Her hair, the colour of straw, hung down around her face in tired wisps. There was hair on her upper lip. She wore a blue sleeveless blouse and pink Bermuda shorts. Her arms were thick and covered with brown freckles.

"What do you want?" she asked.

The false teeth in her mouth gleamed like tombstones in the moonlight. Her eyes swept over him. She couldn't place him and it was annoying her.

"It's about your son Danny," Edge said. "My name is Shannon Edge and I'm from National Insurance."

She nodded towards the house. "I suppose we could go into the verandah," she said.

She pulled up a chair and sat down. "I haven't much time," she said.

"Where is Danny?" Edge asked.

"In New York. He's been there six months now."

"When do you expect him back?" Edge asked.

"Why are you asking me all these questions?"

"There's something missing from his record at the office," Edge said. "We'll need him to come in and give us the information."

"The last time I heard from him," Mrs. Powson said, "he was thinking of extending his stay."

"By the way, is he alone or did he go with a group?"

"Alone," Mrs. Powson said. "His father and I saw him off at the airport."

"When was this?" Edge asked.

"Sometime in May, if I remember correctly."

The little eyes stared at him, confident and sure and a trifle mocking.

"When your son gets back tell him to come and see us," Edge said. "Oh. Have you ever heard of the Columbus Club?"

Mrs. Powson stood up. "Never," she said. "And you've wasted enough of my time."

Edge went back to the car. He deleted Danny Powson's name off of the list that was on his phone. He started the car and drove past the acres of flower gardens and the soft, green lawns. He stopped at the Inn and Out and bought a bottle of beer and a chicken leg. He drove to the beach. He unwrapped the chicken leg, and the sight of it made his stomach heave and he called one of the boys playing on the beach and gave it to him. He drank the beer and sat in the car and stared at the blue-green water. He took out his phone and called Hervey.

Hervey sat in his office as his secretary, Mabel, stood over his shoulder pointing at some papers on his desk. Hervey signed some of the papers as he spoke to Edge through the computer monitor on his desk.

"How is Miss Rowley taking it?"

Edge told him. He also told Hervey about the visit to Mrs. Powson.

Hervey looked at Edge through the monitor and said: "We're keeping an eye on Shelley Hardcastle. She's been out only once. Playing golf again this afternoon."

"What about her phone?"

"Usual routine. We're monitoring her cell, landline and e-mail."

Tapping Shelley's communication devices would save them a lot of legwork, Edge thought.

Using the GPS unit in his car, Edge set a course for Hillaby Village. Cedric Wall lived in Hillaby Village. His name was next on the list.

There are no real mountains in Barbados. From the coastal-plain, the land rises in a series of gentle ridges to the jagged hills in the island's northeast corner. Edge drove slowly through the hot afternoon. He was glad to get away into the countryside, away from the boutiques and packaged fun.

It was cool and green in the interior. This was plantation country, the island's food basket, and green was its colour; the pale green of ripening yams, the golden green of pastureland, and the dark green of banana, breadfruit, avocado and cassava.

Hillaby was just another village on the edge of a ravine. A group of small boys was playing cricket in the road. Edge asked them where Mrs. Wall lived. One of them pointed down a narrow track and showed him a house with a flamboyant tree.

Edge parked the car and got out. The houses were unpainted. They huddled together as though seeking consolation from each other against the poverty and despair that was their lot. There was a radio blaring from every house. A girl with adenoids was singing.

"I only got one desia-h-h-h!"

"And that is to satisfy yah-h-h-h!"

The singing stopped and the disk-jockey began telling his audience what a great lover he was.

Edge knocked on the door of the house. He heard a dog barking somewhere in the back. He knocked again. The dog came around the corner of the house and stopped a few feet away and barked at him. Edge looked at him and he turned away and went and lay down under a tree. A woman came out wiping her hands down the front of her dress.

"Yes?" she said.

"Good afternoon, Mrs. Wall," Edge said. "My name is Edge. I'm from National Insurance and I want to talk to you for a few minutes."

She studied him for several seconds. "I busy getting these children dinner," she said. "But come. You goin' have to talk to me in the kitchen though."

It was hot and cramped in the kitchen. Virginia Wall was frying flying-fish. She took the pan off the stove and placed the fish in a dish and put the pan back and floured four more fish and put them in the pan. She turned to face Edge.

"National Insurance you said?"

"It's about Cedric actually," he said. "Where is he now and when do you expect him back?"

Virginia Wall stepped away from the stove and wiped her face with the hem of her apron.

"I don't want to talk about Cedric," she said.

She was tall, with hard, angular features, hollow cheeks and sunken eyes. It was hard to guess her age, but he knew the grey in her hair had come early. Her dress had been blue originally. She wore rubber slippers.

"He is your husband," Edge said. "The father of your children?"

Her smile was tight and a trifle bitter. "You listen to me," she said. "Cedric walked out of this house a year ago to get a doctor for one of these children. He ain't get back yet. I hear he in America. I don't know."

"How many children do you have?"

"Eight living," she said. She took the pan off the stove and turned the fish. "They all at school."

"Have you seen him lately?" Edge asked. "Where does he live?"

"I does send the biggest boy to him for money when the Saturday come," Virginia Wall said. "Well this is over two months now the children ain't get a cent from he."

"I'd appreciate it if you'd give me his present address," Edge said.

"Go in Nelson Street," she said. "He have a whore there. She name Broadway."

"Where do you work?" Edge asked.

"I doin' a little evening job at the Copa Beach Hotel," she said. "It ain't much but I does try and make it do."

"I guess I'll have to go and see this Broadway," Edge said.

He took a hundred dollars from his pocket. He folded the money in half and held it out to her. She searched his face and he saw the suspicion in her eyes.

"Buy something for the children," he said.

She shook her head. "You don't owe me anything," she said.

I know," Edge said. "But still take it. For the kids."

She took the money and put it on the table. "Tell me," she said. "Is Cedric in trouble?"

"No," Edge said. "Not that I know of."

She stared at him hard. "Be honest with me," she said.

"Honest," Edge said.

He looked back once as he walked down the gap. She was at the window staring after him. Life, he thought, can be a son-of-a-bitch.

Chapter 8

Hunting Leopards

Somebody must've had one hell of a sense of humour, Edge thought. A statue of Lord Nelson – the first to be raised in the British Empire – stands guard at the top of Broad Street and the street where the whores hang out is called Nelson Street.

He stopped at one of the bars near the top of the street. A group of men was leaning against the counter sharing a bottle of Old Brigand rum. Music came from a jukebox in the corner. Two boys in their early teens were playing with a video game machine near the far wall. The man behind the counter asked Edge what he could do for him. Edge told him he was looking for a girl named Broadway.

"Comrade," the man said. "Is rum I selling. Not woman."

"Stop giving the man a hard time, Gus." It was one of the men with the Old Brigand.

"It's important," Edge said.

"Since when whores that important?" the man asked.

"Try Nancy's Parlour up the road, friend," the other man said, and turned back to the rum.

Edge told him thanks. The sun was down. A warm wind gusted in from the sea stirring the crowns of the giant coconut trees that towered above the buildings. A stereo system erupted up the street. Edge hummed a few bars of the calypso under his breath. A truck pulled up in front of him. The men on their way home from work in one of the quarries, by the look of them, jumped down and filed into one of the shops. He heard a man call for a bottle of Cockspur rum.

A light was burning above the door to Nancy's Parlour. A man and a woman stood just inside the doorway talking softly. They stepped back and let Edge through.

The woman at the bar was reading a comic book. Four women and a man sat at a table near the window. Another man sat by himself in a corner drinking rum and coke. The woman put down the comic book and looked at Edge.

"How's Tarzan this evening?" he asked her.

She laughed. A woman got up from the table and went to the jukebox and selected a booming hip-hop song, and went back to the group.

"I only here passing the time here 'til the people start coming," the woman behind the bar said. "I take 'way this thing from my son this morning. I ain't able with Tarzan, nuh! I like my love stories."

"More fun than ape-men," Edge said.

"I don't remember you in here before," the woman said.

"I really came looking for a woman named Broadway," Edge said.

"Let me see if she in," the woman said. She left the room, and when she came back there was another woman with her. She had large breasts and narrow hips. She moved with the slow swaying gait of the female predator. Edge felt her sensuality reach out and pluck at him.

"You want me?" she asked.

Edge tapped the stool next to him. "Sit down," he said.

Her dress was already too short, and as she climbed on to the stool, it shot up around her hips. Edge saw long, firm legs and green lace panties.

"Drink?" Edge asked.

"Vodka and orange juice," she said.

Edge ordered rum and coconut water for himself. The drinks came. He could see her studying him in the glass behind the bar.

"Got a cigarette?"

Edge shook his head.

"Buy me a pack, honey."

The cigarettes came. Edge lit one for her. She pulled the smoke in and blew it at the ceiling.

"You just killing time, or you looking for some action?" she asked him.

"I came looking for action."

"Okay, let's go then. I got a feeling this is going to be one of my busy nights."

Edge paid the bill.

"Give the girl another twenty dollars," Broadway said. "For the bed."

The woman took the money and put it in a tin and put the tin under the counter. Broadway linked her arm through Edge's and walked him through the door marked 'Private'. She pulled open a door halfway down the corridor, and went inside. The room had a bed, a chair, a washstand with a basin and a towel. Broadway stepped out of her slippers. She shrugged her shoulders twice and the dress fell to the floor. Her bra matched her panties and seemed insufficient for the job it was asked to do. She came over to Edge and rubbed against him. She stepped back and ran her hands down her ribs and rested them on her hips.

She smiled at him. "Forty dollars," she said. "Not that I don't trust you. But a girl likes to be sure."

Edge gave her the money. She counted the money and put it on the chair. She walked over to Edge and began unbuttoning his shirt.

"Sit down," he said.

"Now look," Broadway said. "Don't come on with that crap about what a girl like me doing in a place like this. I like what I do and I prefer to get paid for it."

"I know. I want to talk about Cedric."

Broadway sat down on the bed. "Oh him," she said.

"When was the last time you saw him?"

"Are you a policeman?"

"No. I'm just a man who needs help."

Her brows came together and the corners of her mouth drooped.

"Cedric went to New York about six months ago," she said. "He ain't call or e-mail me since he get there."

"Did he tell you why he was going? Where did he get the money?"

"You got to pay for that kind of information," she said suddenly.

Edge handed her twenty. She spread it down on the bed and smoothed it out with her fingers.

"He used to be with something call the Columbus Club. I think he say the club was sending him."

"Did he say why the club was sending him?" Edge asked.

"He say he was just going for a visit."

"Did he say anything else?"

"No, Cedric don't talk much."

Broadway leaned back on the bed. She raised both legs in the air, and opened and shut them like a pair of shears.

"That's all the info I got," she said. "Why not come over here and spend the rest of your money?"

"Some other time perhaps," Edge said.

She drew her legs up. She crossed one knee over the other and her smile mocked him.

She put on her clothes and switched off the light. "Come again when you are not on business," she said.

They went out through the door marked 'Private'.

A man pushed away from one of the tables and stood in front of Edge.

"You overstayed," the man said. "We don't give it away for nothing."

"You're in the way," Edge said.

"I see," the man said. "One of the tough ones." He looked over his shoulder. "The brother's heavy," he said to the men behind him. Just for that I'll take all your cash and your watch."

Edge smiled at him. The man's hand came out of his pocket with a cutthroat razor.

"I'm goin' cut them off of you, big man," he said and went into a crouch.

"So you've been watching the late show," Edge said.

Edge was smiling when he picked up a chair and broke it across the man's back. The man dropped to his knees.

Edge hit him again. The razor slipped from his fingers.

Edge brought his heel down on it and it broke into little pieces. He turned to face the other men.

"Anybody else?" he called softly.

Nobody moved. Nobody said anything. Edge dropped the piece of chair he was holding. He walked out the door and down the steps.

The lights were on in Nelson Street. The night people were out. Men in skin-tight pants minced their way along the pavement. Women waited in doorways and near the mouths of dimly lit alleys, and others, younger, bolder, stalked the night like hunting leopards in mini-skirted packs.

Chapter 9

Limbo

A woman out walking with her husband and her dog showed Edge where Avery-Simms lived. He drove through the double gates and parked the car near the foot of the steps. A woman in an apron and cap came out on the verandah.

"You want somebody?" she called down to him.

Edge went up the steps. "I'm looking for Avery-Simms," he said.

"Who is the body?"

"Edge. Shannon Edge."

She went inside and came back and told him to follow her. John Wendell Avery-Simms sat in his study wiping a gun with an oil rag.

"Mr. Edge," he said. "I've been expecting you. Sit down."

Edge sat down. "So you've been expecting me," he said. "How nice."

Avery-Simms put down the rag. He pointed the gun at Edge. Edge stopped breathing. His lips tightened as he stared into the muzzle of the gun. He watched Avery-Simms's finger take up the pressure on the trigger. Avery-Simms put the gun down and laughed.

"Empty," he said. "I made some inquires about you. You're not with the police. That leaves two other possibilities. You're either a troublemaker or an undercover person. I think it is the latter."

Avery-Simms leaned back and regarded Edge thoughtfully. He was a big man, with a pink face and washed-out blue eyes. His iron-grey hair, brushed high in front, and parted on the right, curled gracefully above his ears and ended just where his collar began. His accent was fake British.

"Strange," Edge said. You don't look dumb to me."

"Okay. I'm sorry about the gun. I heard you were good. I wanted to see your reaction."

"How did you know I was coming to see you?"

"Mary Powson. We've been friends for a long time. I hear that you are interested in the Columbus Club."

"I want to ask some questions," Edge said. "Trouble is there's no one around to answer them. The secretary has disappeared, and so have the records. And as soon as you mention the name, people freeze over like a Canadian winter."

Avery-Simms drew a box of cigars towards him. He selected one and lit it with a gold plated lighter. He pushed the box towards Edge. Edge shook his head. Avery-Simms closed the box and pushed it to one side.

"I don't see why they should. From what George tells me, the club does a little music, plays a little bridge and sometimes takes its members on what it calls cultural tours. If not exactly uplifting, at least quite harmless."

"Harmless clubs just don't go underground," Edge said.

"Perhaps the thing just died," Avery-Simms said. "Clubs have died before."

"What is George doing in New York?"

Avery-Simms studied the tip of his cigar. "I hope he is on holiday," he said thoughtfully.

"What do you mean hope?"

"Don't misunderstand me. George is a good son. Always responsible and all that, but since he became involved with this Prometheus X nut, he's been a changed man." He raised his eyes to Edge's. "You know this Prometheus character?" he asked. Edge said he didn't.

"He's a menace," Avery-Simms continued. "Calls himself a socialist. I think he's a Communist. He holds rallies calling for the downfall of the system. An end to capitalism. He has the rabble all excited. Frankly I don't see how the government can allow that type of behaviour, but it is a free country, I suppose. George has become infected with his philosophy, I'm afraid," Avery-Simms said sadly. "He refers to me as a member of the exploiting class, who grinds the faces of the poor into the ground."

Avery-Simms's cigar had gone out. He lit it again. "George left for New York suddenly, about six months ago," he said. "Said he wanted a holiday. Well at least he's away from that nut and all that talk of reform."

"Have you heard from him since he left?"

"No. But I wish I had."

Edge looked around the study. It was a big comfortable room with heavy, expensive furniture and curtains that reached to the floor.

"Do you agree with your son about being one of those that exploits the poor?"

Avery-Simms smiled, the nice quiet smile of a man who was being perfectly frank.

"I do not," he said quietly. "I am not the grandson of a plantation owner. My people arrived in Barbados over 300 years ago. We were transported from England as indentured labourers. You see, we backed the wrong side at Sedgemoor and lost ourselves the duchy that had been in the family since anybody could remember. After my ancestor served his time at the plantation, he joined a boat that used to bring salt-fish from Halifax. Later he bought his own boat and traded up and down the islands."

Avery-Simms crushed his cigar in the ashtray on the desk.

"My companies employ over three thousand people," he said. "And I treat them all well. It is hard work that put us where we are today, that is why it hurts me so to hear my son call me one of the exploiting class."

Edge stood up. "I won't take any more of your time," he said. "You've been very helpful."

Avery-Simms followed him to the door. "I wish I could tell you more," he said.

A car swung through the gate and came up the driveway. A woman got out and came up the steps.

"Did you have your dinner dear?" she said as she came on. "Sorry I'm late, but the meeting dragged on so. I honestly don't know why Beverley doesn't do something about all the bitching and cackling that goes on."

She looked up and saw Edge. "It's all right dear," Avery-Simms said. "Mr. Edge was just leaving."

"Goodnight, Mrs. Avery-Simms," Edge said as he went by. Constance Avery-Simms didn't answer. Her eyes went right through him.

Edge put the car in the garage. He unlocked the door and went inside. The housekeeper had been in. She had cooked dolphin and breadfruit and left it in the oven. Edge poured a rum and coconut water, and took it with him into the shower. He ate supper. He was listening to Wagner's 'Gotterdammerung' and thinking about Avery-Simms when the phone rang. It was Hervey.

"Shelley Hardcastle called," he said. "She's meeting her brother at the Lilly Pad at one o'clock."

Edge looked at his watch. It was eleven.

"I'll be there," he said.

Edge parked the car in the lot behind the Lilly Pad, and went around the front. The man at the door took fifteen dollars from him. The club was constructed around an open courtyard. The open side faced the sea. Three stunted coconut trees at the end of the courtyard stirred lazily in the breeze.

Edge found an empty table. A waiter came. He ordered a rum and coconut water. On the bandstand, under the flashing lights, six gaunt young men were screaming their way through a recent calypso hit. Edge sipped his drink.

The singing stopped and now there was only the thumping of the bass and the drums. The tourists were bumping, grinding and having a good time as they twirled under the stars. They had come to Barbados for a good time, and by God they were going to have one even if it killed them. Edge finished his drink and ordered another. He checked his phone. He sipped his drink and watched the ladies on the dance floor as the band played in the background. Edge went to the bar.

"I'm meeting a lady here," he said. "But I haven't seen her. I thought perhaps she might have left a message. My name is Edge."

The barman tapped his forehead. "Lemme see," he said. "Yes a lady did phone. That's right, Miss Hardcastle. Said you're to wait here for her."

Edge thanked him and went back to his table. A tall woman came and stood over the table.

"I was afraid I missed you," she said. "Shelley asked me to keep you here until she gets back."

Edge pulled out a chair and she sat down.

"I'm Veronica," she said. "My friends call me Ronnie."

"Hello, Ronnie," Edge said. "I'm Shannon Edge."

"I know," Ronnie said. "Shelley told me. I hope she comes, I need a ride home."

"Known Shelley long?"

"We went to the same school," Ronnie said. "But I know Charles better."

Ronnie was a tall, big-chested girl with a wig and heavy make-up. The waiter came back. She ordered scotch and soda.

"If Shelley doesn't come I'm going to need a ride home," she said.

"I'll give you a ride home if she doesn't come," Edge said.

The music stopped. The lights went down and there was only moonlight falling softly across the dance-floor. A voice spoke out of the shadows. "Ladies and gentlemen, it's limbo time." A drum rolled, light and slow at first, then heavy and quick, until it seemed just one continuous roll. The drumming stopped. A blue light stabbed from a coconut tree on to the dance floor. Into the glow leaped three figures, a man and two women. The drumming started again. Another light splashed across the floor from the opposite side.

The three dancers set up the limbo pole in the centre of the floor, with the bar three feet off the floor. The drumming filled the room, with the drummer repeating the identical patterns each time, and the audience growing quieter and tighter and sitting forward in their chairs.

Edge glanced at Ronnie. She hadn't touched her drink. She sat hunched forward in her chair with her lips parted. The voice spoke again out of the shadows. "Ladies and gentlemen, this is a human limbo."

The dancers leaped and whirled. The first woman danced up to the bar and leaned back from the waist and inched forward under the bar without raising her feet off the floor. The other dancers followed. The audience applauded.

The bar came down about six inches. The man followed the two women under the bar. The bar came down another foot. The women produced three bottles. The man touched a match to them and the oil soaked stoppers caught fire. The women put two torches down on the other side of the limbo bar and gave the other to the man. He put it on his forehead and danced with it around the floor. He danced up to the bar. He bent back from the knees and touched the back of his head three times on the ground. The flame from the torch bent and flickered as the breeze from the sea leaned against it. With the bottle still on his forehead, the man began inching his way under the bar. Edge watched the heaving breasts and the flashing ebony legs and suddenly, he was in a jungle clearing with the drumming coming out of the shadows and the taste of fear and tension in the air. He shook his head and he was back in a Barbados nightclub watching a floor show.

The man was almost past the bar. Only his shoulders and head remained on the other side. Flame leaped suddenly along the entire length of the bar as the torch touched the bar. A woman screamed. Chairs scraped. The moment of panic passed. The audience watched the oil soaked cloth which had been wrapped around the bar, burning.

The tempo of the drumming changed, becoming slower, more plaintive. The man put out the fire on the bar. He spread a cloth on the ground. The two women lay down on their backs about four feet apart. The man placed the limbo bar across their breasts. Edge heard the people near him suck their breath in through their teeth. All that is missing now, is the chanting of the priests and the wailing of the women, Edge thought. Suddenly, he felt angry. What they were seeing was once a secret and sacred ritual connected with fertility and thanksgiving and the organic integrity of the commonwealth. Now, on the other side of the ocean, it had become a circus attraction with tourists paying pennies to see it.

Nobody moved in the entire audience. There was no sound but the wail of the drum. At a table near Edge, a waiter set down his tray and sat with the guests.

The drumming grew softer. The dancer was moving now as if his body had forgotten its bones. He bent backwards slowly and his back was almost on the ground and he eased himself forward inch by careful inch. He got his legs through, and his torso. The arms came up to steady him and the knees came up, and only his head remained on the other side of the bar. Edge waited for the man to fall backwards. In fact by any standards he ought to have fallen over long before this, but still he moved until his head too passed under the bar. He came upright. He leaped into the air. The women got up. The drumming stopped. The lights came on. Edge heard a sigh wash like a wave over the audience.

Ronnie picked up her glass and emptied it in one gulp.

"That thing's scary," she said.

Edge smiled. He wasn't listening, he was thinking about Shelley Hardcastle.

"Care for another drink?" he asked.

Ronnie shook her head. The music started again. A few couples went on to the floor, then the leader of the band said good night and the people started leaving.

"Where is she? I hope nothing's happened to Shelley," Ronnie said.

"Let's give her another 10 minutes," Edge said.

"I'm going to call her cell to see what's going on," said Ronnie.

Ronnie phoned Shelley but there was no answer. She left a message, smiled uncomfortably at Edge and put the phone back in her purse. Twenty minutes later she still hadn't come.

"I'll give you a ride home," Edge said.

The Volkswagen was the only car left in the parking lot. Ronnie stopped to light a cigarette. Two men came out from behind the car and the warning light that had been flickering in Edge's mind ever since Ronnie came and sat with him suddenly glowed bright red. The moonlight picked up the flash of the knives in the men's hands.

"He isn't carrying a gun," Ronnie said. "And we have the night to ourselves, so do a real good job."

Chapter 10

The Knife Artist

The two men moved apart. The way they moved and the way they held the knives told Edge they were professionals. Edge feinted to the right, moved left and swung his foot in a hard, flat arc at the kneecap of the man nearest to him. The man staggered. Edge stepped inside the man's guard. He caught the man's knife wrist and slammed the edge of his hand into the man's neck just below the ear. The man screamed. Edge stepped behind him still holding his hand. The man was now between Edge and the second attacker. Edge hit him in the same spot. The man's head tilted sideways. Edge pushed him away. The man took two steps forward and crashed on his face.

Edge waited for the other man. The man came up on the balls of his feet, moving in a circle. He leaped suddenly. The knife arched towards Edge's solar plexus. Edge stepped aside. His foot crashed into the man's side just above the kidney. The man staggered. His knees buckled, but he managed to stay on his feet. He swung to face Edge. He was more careful now. He was breathing hard through his mouth. Edge could tell he was in pain. The blow had been a crippling one. The man was sweating. He realized suddenly that it was he and not Edge who was fighting for his life.

Edge feinted to the left and moved right. He saw the knife driving towards him. He knocked the hand down and away. But the knife had been aimed with all the desperate strength of a man about to die. A streak of fire raced along Edge's ribs. He hit the man with the side of his hand just above the top lip. Edge knew that he was dead before he hit the pavement.

He put his hand on the cut on his side. His fingers came away wet. He bit down hard against the pain. He bent and picked up the knife. He looked for Ronnie. She was leaning against the car.

"As for you…" Edge said.

Ronnie stepped away from the car. She smiled at him. Her hands went to her head and the wig came away.

"Looks like I'm going to have to finish the job after all," she said. The voice was a man's. "Don't worry," Ronnie said. "You're going to be dead in a few minutes anyhow."

Ronnie put his hand inside his bosom and took out a switchblade. "Boy am I ever going to enjoy this," he said.

Ronnie came at him fast. Edge jumped back. Ronnie's knife opened his shirt from navel to neck. The knife was everywhere. It was all Edge could do to keep it away from his heart.

Ronnie stepped back. He laughed. He began moving to Edge's left. He switched the knife from right to left. Suddenly Edge was wide open. Ronnie darted in like a cobra. The knife took Edge high in the shoulder.

"I'm going to carve you and watch you die slow, real slow," laughed Ronnie.

A stream of saliva was running down Ronnie's chin. He was panting. Edge knew it was from pleasure. He was going to die the next time Ronnie came at him. Ronnie's blade glistened in the moonlight as he rotated his hand from side to side. Edge saw the point of the knife come up as Ronnie gathered himself for the final lunge. Edge took a few steps back. He balanced the knife between forefinger and thumb. Edge grabbed Ronnie's wrist. The knife was on its way before Ronnie realized what was happening.

A look of reproach flitted across his face during that split-second before the knife went in under the left brassiere-cup. Ronnie screamed like a stricken mare. His fingers clawed at the handle of the knife. He dropped to his knees, remained like that for a few seconds then fell on his face. His pelvis lifted slowly and drove into the ground, once, twice, three times. Then he was still.

Sweat poured down Edge's brow and he dropped to one knee. He gritted his teeth as he struggled to remain conscious. The sound of the ocean waves pounding the shore helped to drown out his laboured breathing. Ronnie's dead body began to blur and fade into darkness.

"Stuck up son-of-a-bitch..." Edge said.

He drove with one hand and he tried to slow the bleeding with the other. Suddenly, he felt very alone. A vision of a big soft woman with kids and hair disheveled floated into his mind. He shook his head. No, he thought. This is the way I want it.

He got out of the car and staggered across the road and knocked on the house. He knocked for a very long time it seemed. Lights came on and the door opened. He stumbled past Fenella Rowley into the house.

"Sorry to get you out of bed," he said.

Darkness spread soft, warm arms out towards him. His phone slipped from his fingers. Fenella became wavy about the edges.

"Here," she said. "Let me help you."

Her voice fetched him back and he held on to her with all of his strength.

"Tell me the number," she said.

"Hervey...I've tried already," Edge whispered. "It's in the phone."

He began to give her Hervey's number and the floor came up and hit him in the face.

He was climbing a rope ladder towards the top of a castle-wall. It was raining hard but he had already climbed too far to turn back. Below him, waves pounded against the base of the wall. He could feel the wall tremble. The ladder swayed wildly with every step he took. He knew he had to keep going. A face appeared on the battlements. It was Franklyn Somerset. He tugged the ladder. Edge tumbled a long, slow somersault down into the sea. He skidded on the water, went under and opened his eyes.

He was in a woman's room. There were rows of jars and bottles and sprays on the bureau near the foot of the bed. The sheets were crisp and clean and smelled of lavender. Edge closed his eyes and tried to remember where he was. He gave it up and sat up. The pain hit him and he remembered. The door opened. Fenella came in.

"Hi!" she said. "How's the conquering hero this morning?"

"Don't make fun of me," Edge said. "I'm fragile and I might break."

"You don't look fragile to me," she said. "And fragile your language certainly isn't. Last night was a different story. The doctor your friend Hervey sent couldn't believe you actually drove here in your condition."

Edge was shirtless and he ran his fingers across the bandages that covered his wounds. Fenella sat on the edge of her bed and smiled at him. Fenella was barefooted. Her sleeveless dress had vertical blue and white stripes. It was tied at the waist with a cord of the same material. She wasn't wearing a bra. She looked freshly scrubbed.

"I'm sorry to be such a nuisance," Edge said. "But as I stood there watching my blood form little pools on the ground, I couldn't seem to think of anyone but you."

"Watch it," she said. "I'm fragile too." There was sadness in her voice.

"What time is it?"

"One thirty."

Edge looked at the bed. Both pillows had been slept on. Fenella's eyes followed the direction of his glance. She shrugged.

"Don't worry about it," she said. "I was outside on the couch, but you kept tossing and swearing, and I got worried about you. I think you must've been cold. As soon as I lay down beside you and put your head on my chest you fell asleep."

Edge took her hand. "That must've been when I was dreaming I was in heaven," he said. He became serious. "The first moment I get, I'm taking you out to dinner," he said.

Fenella said: "You don't owe me anything. Now if you'll let go of my hand, I'll go and fix your breakfast."

Meyers stood in the doorway to Fenella's room. He was leaning against the door frame.

"C'mon Edge," he said. "There was a time when you didn't have to get stabbed to spend the night in a woman's bed."

Edge sat up on the edge of the bed as Fenella walked towards Meyers to leave the room.

"I'll give you two some privacy," said Fenella. "Breakfast will be on the table when you're ready."

"How did you get here?" asked Edge.

"Hervey's orders," Meyers said. "I arrived with the doctor. Hervey thought you might need me to hold your hand when you woke up."

"Fenella could do a better job."

"Uh-huh! Hervey thought of that too," Meyers said. He closed the door and dropped into a chair.

"Your jousting session last night made the paper," Meyers said. "They printed that a cross-dresser was attacked by two thugs and everyone ended up killing each other. I didn't know you were that good."

"Not good," Edge said. "Lucky."

"Special Branch checked out Shelley Hardcastle's story," Meyers said. "She was waiting at the Lilly Pad, and Charles called again and said to meet him in the car park outside the Canadiana, but he never showed."

"And Fenella?"

"Under house-arrest. Hervey's orders."

Edge's phone began to ring. He gingerly reached for it as it lay on the night table beside him.

"I wonder who that could be?" said Edge. He picked up the phone and answered it. Hervey's face appeared on the screen.

"Hi, Hervey."

Hervey said: "When are you going to do some work? You're not being paid to lie on your back."

"In about a week or ten days," Edge said.

Hervey gave no sign that he heard what Edge said. "Avery-Simms is dead," he said.

"Murder or suicide?"

"The maid was getting ready to leave for the night when she heard what sounded like a shot," Hervey said. "When she opened the study door, she saw him slumped forward on the desk with a gun in his hand and a hole in his head."

"Did he leave a note or anything?" Edge asked.

"No, and there's no reason why he should want to take his own life, according to his widow," Hervey said.

"He must've learned that George is dead," Edge said.

"I expect so," said Hervey.

"I hear Miss Rowley is under house-arrest."

"She's not under house-arrest," Hervey said. "I merely suggested to her that she remain indoors during the course of your confinement there. Until this investigation is concluded everyone is suspect. And really, it's your fault for running to her."

"I was going to do a security check first, but it slipped my mind," Edge said.

Hervey ignored the sarcasm. "Sub-conscious mother-fixation," he growled. "You get your feelings hurt and you run looking for comfort. You were lucky. Miss Rowley is a resourceful woman."

"You did a check on her I suppose."

"I did. Her brother could've been planting that bomb in your car when it went off and killed him," Hervey said.

"I know you're supposed to be paranoid, but isn't that a little far out?"

"I don't believe things," Hervey said. "I check and find out. Now go back to sleep, you're still light-headed. I'll call you at four."

Edge put down the phone. Meyers smiled at him and told him he would check on him later. As Meyers headed out of the room, Fenella came in with the day's paper.

"To give your spirits a lift," she said. She went out.

Edge glanced at the pages. In the United States of America, there was debate on how to tackle the financial crisis that had gripped them, and much of the world. At home the seven Independence Beauty Queen contestants had all pronounced themselves "nervous but confident", and the wife of an expatriate bank manager had mislaid a Pekingese named 'Porridge' and was offering a small sum for its return. The story made the front page.

Edge awoke at five o'clock. He showered. Fenella changed the bandages on his wounds. His ribs and his shoulder hurt. Fenella had laid out on the bed, the clothes Meyers had brought him. He put his arms through the sleeves of the shirt and the pain flared suddenly. He swore through clenched teeth and checked for signs of bleeding, found none and pushed the pain to the back of his mind.

"I'll get the car," Meyers said. He went out.

Fenella came into the room. "You're going," she said. She was trying to smile.

"Yes," Edge said. "In a few minutes." He closed the suitcase and turned to face her. "You've been very kind," he said. "Thanks."

"Any time," she said. She put her hand into her pocket and took out a small bottle. "The doctor said you should take these tablets."

He took the bottle from her and put it in his shirt pocket. He drew her close to him and kissed her softly on the mouth. She let her head fall on his chest.

"Promise me something, Shannon," she said softly.

He lifted her chin with one finger. He felt her shudder against him.

"Don't let them hurt you anymore," she whispered.

"I'll be careful," he said. "And I'm sorry for all the bother I've caused you."

She laughed. There was sadness in it. "You know where I live. The door is open. I'd love you to come back."

He bent and brushed her lips. "I'll be back," he said. "Good luck."

He drew the back of his right hand down her left cheek. "Take care," he said. "And keep the cane juice cool until I see you again."

Hervey came around the desk. He said: "How is the wound?" He didn't wait for Edge to answer. "Shelley is meeting her brother in a few minutes," he continued. "There is a car outside waiting for you."

Edge pulled up a chair and sat down. There was a stiffness along his left side and his shoulder ached every time he moved it.

"I need a gun," he said.

Hervey looked off in the distance. "The Minister said no guns."

"He's afraid they might go off and scare the tourists," Edge said. "That's his problem. Mine is staying alive."

Hervey filled out a requisition form and passed it to Edge.

"The keys are in the car," he said.

Edge went down to the cellar. He knocked on the door marked 'Supplies'. The door opened and Cyril Parks grinned at him.

"You come in for some practice?" he asked Edge.

"No," Edge said. "This is for real."

Parks took the requisition slip. He went to the wall at the back of the room and took down a gun and brought it back to Edge.

"I cleaned it yesterday," Parks said. He gestured towards Edge's middle. "You hurt bad?" he asked.

"A scratch," Edge said. "Thanks for looking after the gun for me."

"You look after yourself now," Parks said.

The gun was a 9mm SIG Sauer P226. Edge checked the magazine and signed the receipt for the gun and fifty rounds of ammunition. The car was Special Branch. The Bureau couldn't afford Infiniti G37's on its budget. Somebody had put in a lot of work with a polish cloth. Edge started the car and pulled out into the street. He switched on the radio and heard a woman's voice warning the other Special Branch cars to stand by. Edge wondered if she was the same woman who had given Meyers and himself the ride back from the beach. He pressed a button on the car's steering wheel and told her he was standing by.

Shelley was driving west on Bay Street. The woman gave him the description and the license number of the car. Shelley turned down a side street. The first car went by and the second one picked her up. Twenty minutes later the second car handed her over to Edge. Shelley drove quietly, not even bothering to check the rear-view mirror. Edge allowed two cars to come between them. He stayed back until Shelley pulled into the parking lot of the Copacabana Hotel. He took up the radio and told the other cars to go home.

Edge went through the lobby. The receptionist was on the phone. Judging from her gestures and expression, the gossip she was sharing was particularly juicy. No point asking her about Shelley, Edge thought. An illuminated elephant could have walked past without her seeing it. He took the stairs two at a time. He swerved around two women in short, tight skirts who were walking in the middle of the stairway. He reached the top of the stairs in time to see Shelley disappear around a corner. Edge hurried after her. He heard a man and a woman coming along the corridor behind him. The man sounded drunk.

"The key, honey," the woman said. "Give baby the key, honey."

The man had a bottle of rum in his hand. The woman was about nineteen. She had a reddish Afro. The man mumbled something. The woman said: "You sure this is the room?"

Edge turned the corner after Shelley and saw her slip into one of the rooms. The sound of a heavy fall came from the corridor behind Edge. He hesitated, then went back. The man lay on his back with his mouth open. The woman bent over him. She rolled him over on his face and started going through his pockets. Her dress was smooth and tight across her behind. Edge knew she was not wearing anything underneath. She found the wallet and straightened up.

"Naughty," Edge said. "Naughty."

The woman whirled to face him. "Mind your own business," she snapped.

Edge held out his hand. "Give," he said quietly.

"I'll split it with you. Fifty-fifty."

"I want it all," Edge said.

She inhaled slowly. Edge saw the kick coming. It came at the groin, a fast crippling blow thrown by a woman who had done that sort of thing before. Edge leaned forward and caught her heel. He jerked the foot forward and up. She hit the floor on her back with her feet in the air.

He picked the wallet up off the floor. The woman got to her feet and tugged the dress down around her thighs. She waited for her breath to come back. She began to tell Edge about his mother and grandmother. He smiled at her. She spat at him and turned on her heel and walked away down the corridor.

Edge found the key in the man's pocket. He unlocked the door. He carried the man into the room and put him on the bed. He put the wallet on the table near the rum and keys. He went out, and pulled the door shut. He went along the corridor and knocked on the door of the room where Shelley was, and waited.

Chapter 11

Prometheus X

A voice said: "Leave it outside the door."

The door opened. Edge leaned against it and the man stumbled backwards into the room. He was naked except for a towel around his middle. A woman was on the bed. She threw Edge a startled glance and dived under the sheet. The man backed away until he hit the wall. He raised a hand as if to ward off a blow. His mouth worked but no sound came.

"I'm sorry," Edge said. "I came to the wrong room."

The man found his voice. It was a little more than a croak. "I ought to kick your ass," he said.

"Do that and your towel will fall off," Edge said.

The man grabbed the towel with both hands. His mouth clicked shut.

"Relax," Edge said. "I'm not her husband."

He went out and closed the door behind him. I hope I didn't spoil anything for them, he thought. He leaned against a wall and waited. He waited for about fifteen minutes.

A door opened and Shelley came out. She saw him. Her hand went to her mouth.

"You followed me," she said.

"Yes," Edge said. "Now tell Charles to open the door."

Her eyes searched his face. She reached for his hands. "Don't hurt him," she said. "He's gone through a lot these past few days. I don't think he can take much more."

"I only want to talk to him," Edge said.

"Be gentle with him. Please? For my sake?"

She called to Charles through the door. The door opened. Charles Hardcastle was sitting on the edge of the bed. He needed a shave. The room stank of alcohol, cigarette smoke and stale sweat. Charles passed his hands over his face. His fingers were shaking. Shelley went to him and put her arms around him.

"I'm sorry," she said. "It's my fault they found you."

"It doesn't matter anymore," Charles said.

Edge sat on the corner of the dresser. He looked around the room. The curtains hung limp. The walls were bleak and cheerless. Disappointment, frustration and despair screamed at him from the four corners.

"Something tells me there isn't much time," Edge said. "You talk, I'll listen."

"The Columbus Club was a fine idea that went wrong," Hardcastle said.

Shelley slid along the bed away from Charles. She gave herself a cigarette and looked at Edge through the smoke.

"The original idea was to do some dance, drama, debating, that sort of thing," Hardcastle continued. "Then the political activists joined. And in no time at all they had the club framing manifestos. I knew we had been infiltrated, but I guess I felt the remaining members of the old guard might somehow get things straight again."

Charles motioned to Shelley. She lit a cigarette and stuck it in his mouth.

"But that group belonged to Prometheus X," Charles continued. "And as it turned out, they were looking for a harmless organization to use as a front. A few security people even joined the club to keep an eye on things. That's when I decided to get out."

"About the trip to the U.S., who organized that?"

"George Avery-Simms produced a letter inviting a group from the club to visit the U.S. as guests of a cultural group in New York," Hardcastle said. "A committee was appointed to choose five people and the committee appointed itself. This got the other members very angry and the club folded soon afterwards."

"So you went into hiding," Edge said. "Why?"

"I got this call early one morning. The caller said the police was investigating the Columbus Club and that there were going to be arrests under the Public Order Act. I got scared because I knew some people in the club had been openly preaching violence."

"When was this call?"

"The same morning you came to the house."

Edge came off the dresser. "You don't need to hide anymore," he said. "Go home and get some sleep."

"You mean you're not going to arrest me?"

"Somebody was pulling your leg," Edge said.

Shelley came over to Edge and put her hand on his chest. "When are you coming to see me?" she asked.

"This business should blow over in a couple of days," Edge said. "Then I'll be coming to see you."

"I'll keep the champagne cool for you."

"Make it rum. And if you can get a little coconut water, keep it nearby."

Shelley stood on her toes and kissed him. "You're terribly sweet. Do you know that?"

Edge laughed. "Women tell me that all the time," he said.

"Yes, I bet they do," Shelley said. "Well, look after yourself, and don't forget our date."

Charles said: "I feel better already. Seems like confession is really good for the soul."

Edge opened the door and went out. He smiled at the receptionist, and she gave him one in return. It was warm outside, and the sky was deep indigo except where the rays of the sun reached up from beyond the horizon, and tinted the clouds pink. Edge took out his phone and searched the internet for any information regarding Prometheus X. His search took him to Prometheus X's webpage. There was going to be a meeting that evening at eight o'clock in Independence Square.

Edge parked the car about half a mile away, and walked back through the crowd to Independence Square. The man who called himself Prometheus X stood on the platform of a truck under a light. He was a brown-skinned black man, with a beard, dreadlocks and glasses. He wore jeans and slippers, and an old button-down shirt with the sleeves rolled back to the elbows. He leaned in close to the microphone. His voice, gentle and controlled, lashed his listeners like a whip wrapped in velvet.

"Listen and you hear laughing," he was saying. "People are laughing at you in London, New York and in Toronto. Laughing at the joke you call independence." The crowd leaned close to catch his words in spite of the two amplifiers and the monumental hush that was over everything.

"Fanon called independence conferences 'meetings to confirm the property rights of the ruling classes'," he continued. "That's what your leaders went to Britain to do. You think you have freedom? Economic freedom? When the papers for independence were signed all those years ago," he was saying, "your leaders went to Britain to confirm the property rights of the ruling classes. They signed a paper saying that the banks and plantations and insurance companies will remain forever the property of the slave owners. And tomorrow, you will be jumping up and down celebrating that betrayal. No wonder they are laughing in the northern capitals."

Prometheus X folded his arms across his chest. The crowd was silent, waiting.

"The bunch of clowns you call leaders have sold you," he said quietly. "We have been sold for decades. On the eve of another Independence Anniversary, you are as much a slave as your great grandfathers were! Nobody can give you freedom. Freedom, economic or otherwise, can't be given to you. Freedom isn't something you can put in a Colonial Office folder and hand to people. You got to fight for real freedom. That is our trouble. We never fought for freedom and you ain't got none."

He told the people the country was poor, and that it was poor because each year millions of dollars went out of the country. Money the exploiters called profits, but which was really money stolen from the working-class, since if the companies paid an honest wage, there would be no profits to send to Canada, England and the U.S.A.

Edge had heard it before, but never from a political platform in Barbados. Prometheus's message was one that was being echoed throughout the streets of the Western world where financial ruin seemed to be around the corner. He moved closer. Prometheus X stood with one hand grasping the microphone and the other thrust into the pocket of his jeans, eyes blazing, teeth flashing, half madman, half martyr, on a collision course with history.

Prometheus X paused. When he spoke again his voice was quieter and there was a sadness in it.

"They call me a communist and anarchist," he said. "Let them. They can jail me. I ain't afraid! I believe with Thoreau that in a land of dishonest men the only place for an honest man is in jail. I ain't 'fraid jail. I ain't 'fraid to die! Your Prime Minister can do what he like. You ever see a white domestic servant? Or a white beggar? Or a white taxi man? Why not? Because they got more brain than you? No way. Is because they white. Because this is a racist country. An' is your politicians keeping it so. The Man say he abolish slavery, but that is only a trick. He ain't abolish nothing. You got paper independence but that is all."

A group of young men near the platform raised their arms and shouted: "Power to the people!" The shouting died away.

Prometheus X said: "Power must return to the hands of the people where it belongs. All power is given unto you the people. Even the oppressor says the voice of the people is the voice of God. Power to the people! Power to the people!"

There was silence for a few seconds. The young men near the platform began chanting: "Power to the people! Power to the people!" The crowd picked up the cry until the chant filled the square.

Edge glanced at the faces near him. Some people were not saying anything. Their faces, however, mirrored the terror and fascination of agnostics at a revival meeting.

Prometheus raised his hands. The chanting died away.

"It takes more than noise to start a revolution," he said. He had not moved and his voice was quiet as ever. "Revolution calls for action and we're either part of the revolution or part of the reaction. We have to free ourselves, and any act that gives this present repressive system a kick in the ass, is an act of revolution, and a noble act. Decide what you are going to do, but for God's sake do something." He paused. "I know what I am going to do," he continued slowly. "I am going to spread this message every minute of the day, every day of my life until the people own every blade of cane, every hotel, every grain of sand and every drop of water in this country. And if I have to die, then I will die."

Before the cheering stopped, Edge heard people running up Fairchild Street. There was shouting and the sound of glass breaking. A police siren wailed in the distance.

Prometheus X sat on the platform of the truck chatting with a group of his supporters, watching the crowd drift away.

"They are breaking windows in Fairchild Street," a man near Prometheus X said.

"Let them," Prometheus X said.

"Aren't you over-working the Frantz Fanon a little bit?" Edge asked.

Prometheus X raised one hand and the conversation died. He looked Edge up and down.

"A policeman," he said. "One of the protectors of the ruling class."

Four young men came forward and stood between Edge and Prometheus X. Prometheus X waved them away.

"Let him through," he said. The men broke ranks and Edge passed through.

"I want to talk to you," he said.

"I can't tell you anything that isn't already on file in the Security Division of the Prime Minister's Office," Prometheus X said.

"This is different."

"I'm listening."

"Privately."

There was a murmur from the men around Prometheus X. "Relax," he said. "I want to hear this Brother out."

He jumped down from the truck and took Edge's arm. Suddenly he said: "Smile, you're on camera."

Edge saw a man in an old jacket and worn runners point something at them. It was the same type of camera phone that Edge had gotten from the Bureau.

"Your people," Prometheus X continued. "I'm thinking of charging them a fee for my services."

They stopped underneath an almond tree at the other end of the square. The bodyguards waited a little way off.

"You're about the most dangerous man in Barbados right now," Edge said.

"If I am, it is because I am not afraid," Prometheus X said.

"The question is why are you not in jail?"

"I'm not a terrorist. The Prime Minister is afraid of a political trial. He is posing as the big father figure, and he wants to remain the people's friend, so he can't arrest the people's champion. He knows I'll turn it into a political trial."

"You seem very sure of yourself," Edge said. "That kind of confidence makes people careless."

"It doesn't matter. Leaders come and go, but the people live on," Prometheus X said. "The important thing is to fire them up with an idea."

"Five men came ashore at Barracuda Reef a few nights ago," Edge said slowly. "They had automatic weapons and plastic explosives. Were they part of firing up the people with an idea?"

Prometheus X was still for about ten seconds. He said: "Say that again. Are you telling me that there are guerrillas on the island?"

"I was there. I saw them come ashore."

"And you killed them."

"They're dead," Edge said.

"That figures. Or else you wouldn't be here."

"Don't play games," Edge said wearily. "When they didn't turn up, you knew they had to be dead."

"You asshole," Prometheus X said. "So that's your game." He leaned in close so that Edge could see the anger in his eyes and the smell of tobacco on his breath. "You come here with a dumb story about men on a beach so that you can accuse me of having foreign connections. Well go back to the people who own you and tell them it ain't goin' to work. I don't need no help from outside. My army is the oppressed people of this country and when your Prime Minister gets the kick in his ass, it will be from them and not from foreigners."

"Ever thought of going in for acting? You'd make a fortune," Edge said.

Prometheus X shook his head. "It won't work," he said quietly. "Tell Franker if he's planning to produce a few rusty guns and tell people that he's uncovered a plot against his government, I Prometheus X will construe that as an act of war against the people, and he will be responsible for the consequences."

"Rhetoric won't help," Edge said. "The evidence is there and it's hard to beat. If you got any private business to look after do it quickly. You're going to be in jail before this time tomorrow."

Something flickered in Prometheus X's eyes. He forced a laugh. "You're trying to scare me," he said. "But I don't scare easy." There was something in his voice that wasn't there before. Edge waited.

"That yacht out in the bay," Prometheus X said. "That mine too? I hear they very cosy with Government."

"I hear it is on a Caribbean cruise."

"Caribbean cruise my ass," Prometheus X said. Prometheus reached into his pocket for his phone.

Prometheus X showed Edge a picture on his phone. It was Steele and Thomas Bunker Hill on Hill's yacht. "I saw your friend Steele go aboard with a few of the ruling class. Whenever you see a Cracker bastard and Barbadian big shots hobnobbing, the masses gwine get their asses kick."

"And it's your job to save them."

"You wouldn't understand," Prometheus X said. "You've already been bought and paid for."

Chapter 12

The McCool Woman

The phone woke Edge. He picked it up without opening his eyes. It was Hervey.

"Prometheus X has been arrested," Hervey said. "Get down here as soon as you can."

Edge put down the phone. He swung his legs off the bed and went to the washroom. He came out and gave himself a bottle of beer.

"Cooper sent me this file by special courier," Hervey said.

Edge sat down. It was six o'clock. The wind that came in off the streets was still fresh and cool.

Hervey pushed the file across to Edge and leaned back and looked at the ceiling. Edge opened the file. None of the surprise he felt showed on his face. Prometheus X had been arrested at three this morning on board the Liberty Queen. The police had gone aboard the yacht acting on a tip from an 'undisclosed source'. Prometheus X and the man with him had surrendered without a struggle.

Edge read the final paragraph through twice. "Investigations currently being pursued by the security services have established links between Prometheus X and five men who tried to sneak ashore at Barracuda Reef on the night of the twenty-sixth. The Police also have discovered a plot to abduct the Prime Minister and hold him at some secret place and use him as a hostage to force the Government's surrender. It is known that Prometheus X and his group planned to seize the yacht and hold the Prime Minister there."

Edge pushed the file towards Hervey.

"Well?" Hervey lit a cigarette. He blew a stream of smoke at the window.

Edge didn't say anything. He was looking out the window at the tree tops.

"It would've been nice if the Bureau could've got in there ahead of Special Branch," Hervey said.

Edge wasn't listening. He wondered how long Special Branch had known about the plot. And Prometheus X. There had been something about him. A fire and a conviction as well as an obvious recklessness, but he hadn't struck Edge as the kind of man to pull something as stupid as trying to hijack the Liberty Queen. Which only goes to show you can't take people by their looks, he said to himself. He got up.

"I'm going down to see Cooper," he said.

The door of Cooper's office opened and Prometheus X came in flanked by two policemen. Cooper waved the policemen outside. The policemen went out and closed the door behind them. Prometheus X was in the same clothes he had worn when he addressed the meeting. He pulled a chair and sat down, and a bitter smile played around the corners of his mouth.

Cooper flicked a box of Embassy towards him and leaned forward and lit the cigarette. The prisoner drew the smoke deep into his lungs and blew it out through his nose. He looked at Edge and said: "I knew I couldn't be bought. What I forgot is that I could be sold."

"You don't have to sell stupid people," Edge said. "You just leave them alone and they trip over their own stupidity sooner or later." He was angry.

"You were part of the transaction," Prometheus X continued quietly. His voice was sad with the knowledge of defeat. "You fed me a line about people landing here with guns and explosives and I believed it. When I got home, somebody called me and told me this yacht was carrying guns for Franker. I put two and two together, and I work it out that Franker has declared war against the people. There is only one thing for an honest man to do, and that is throw those guns into the sea."

He crushed out his cigarette. He put his hands behind his head and looked up at the ceiling.

"I didn't understand just how deep the corruption runs in this country," he said. His eyes sought and held Edge's. "You set me up for the phone call. There never were any men on that beach."

Edge studied the man opposite him. The defeat that was there like a shadow a moment ago now hung on him like an overcoat.

"I don't know who called you about the yacht," Edge said slowly. "But my guess is that whoever it was must've been a real trusted friend and confidant. Somebody you knew you could trust. I'll give you ten seconds to guess who called the police and told them you were going aboard the Liberty Queen."

Prometheus X seemed to sink further into the chair.

"No," he said softly.

Cooper called through the door. The two policemen came and took the prisoner away.

"The charges against him include being armed with an offensive weapon, attempted hijacking, trespassing and extortion," Cooper said. "Looks like Franker won after all."

Edge's phone rang. "Excuse me, its Hervey."

"The Minister called," Hervey said. "Congratulated the Bureau on a fine job. Had very high praise for you. Wants you to take a few days off. Says you earned it."

"Tell the Minister thanks very much," Edge said.

"Did you get a chance to talk to the prisoner?"

"Yes. He claims someone set him up."

"I hope he can convince the jury," Hervey said. "I hear they intend to throw the book at him. Trouble with those starry-eyed types, is they have too much faith in human nature. Comes from reading all that Marx, I suppose.

Edge put the phone away. He waited until Cooper raised his eyes from the file he was pretending to study.

"Okay," Edge said. "What gives?"

"What are you talking about?"

"Your people set Prometheus X up. Why?"

Cooper leaned back and folded his arms. He nodded towards Edge. "This interests me," he said. "Go ahead."

"Look man." Edge leaned over the desk. "Somebody set him up, and it wasn't us."

Cooper sighed wearily. "When Prometheus X was arrested, I was home in bed," he said slowly. "A sergeant from the Harbour Police made the arrest. Special Branch was not in any way involved. And another thing. We do not set people up."

"Jesus Christ," Edge said. "The man was set up! Who did it?"

"I know who didn't do it," Cooper said.

"Do you know what you just said?"

"Okay, so there's a cell on the island," Cooper said slowly. "Strong enough and arrogant enough to make fun of the security forces. How do you like them apples?"

"Why do they want Prometheus X in jail? And why go to all that trouble?"

Cooper smiled. He was enjoying himself. "Who knows? Maybe Franker is getting ready to move against the Opposition. First the men on the beach, then Prometheus X, now this rumour of a plot to kidnap Franker. Could you blame him if he declared a state of emergency and locked up the Opposition?"

"That's not Franker's style," Edge said. "I don't suppose your people came up with anything on the Boozy story."

"That story was a plant," Cooper said.

"I can hear somebody laughing," Edge said. "And the joke's on us."

He parked the car and went around the front of the bank. The teller gave him her little smile. He wrote out a cheque for two-hundred and fifty dollars. He passed the cheque to her.

"Do I have enough to cover that?" he asked.

She went to the ledgers and came back. She counted out the money and passed it to him. She wrote a figure on a slip of paper and handed it to him. Edge looked at it.

"I think you made a mistake," he said.

The teller spun the computer screen around so Edge could see his account.

"Wire transfer. It came two days ago."

The computer screen showed a balance of over 50 thousand dollars in his account.

"Who sent the money?"

"Crowe, Morgenlau and Mastien, attorneys. The transfer was drawn on the Bank of America."

"Uncle must have remembered me after all," he said.

There was a coldness in the pit of his stomach. He put the money in his pocket and went to the car. Workmen were stringing blue, black and gold Barbados colours along the sides of the building and across the streets. A car passed. Somebody threw a fire-cracker from the window and a few people jumped in the air and someone threw a curse at the back of the car.

Hervey was trying to complete a crossword when Edge walked in.

"Why aren't you at the beach?" he growled at Edge.

"I come from a long line of hard-working people." Edge dropped into a chair. "Don't blame me if I don't know when to stop."

Hervey closed the magazine and said: Harrumph." He got up from behind the desk. "I'm going to see the Prime Minister," he said. "You might as well come along."

Mable Hillier looked up from her computer as they passed. "Mr. Hervey," she said. "There is something here I don't quite understand."

"Leave the draft on my desk," Hervey said. "I think I may have to do another one."

The policeman at the gate waved Hervey's car through. Hervey parked the Jaguar and they went up the steps. A man came across the verandah and waited for them at the top of the steps.

"The Prime Minister is expecting you," he said.

They followed the man inside. The living room was done in blue and gold and dotted with solid-looking antique furniture. The crystal and silver ornaments made Edge think of Scandinavia. On the wall near the door an African drummer leaned above a tall drum and banged his message across the centuries.

The man said: "Your weapons, please, gentlemen."

Edge handed over the Sauer. The man balanced it in his hand and put it on the table.

"Right on through," he said. "The Prime Minister is expecting you."

Franker stood up as they came through the door. "Hello John," he said. He and Hervey shook hands. Hervey introduced Edge.

They were in Franker's study. Bookcases lined three sides of the room. A large picture-window on the other side looked out on the vegetable garden. The door opened and a waiter came in.

"What are you drinking?" Franker asked.

Hervey said scotch and soda. Franker asked for fruit punch. Edge said rum and coconut-water. The drinks came. Franker stood up and proposed a toast to the country. They stood with him and drank. Edge studied Franker over the rim of his glass. He saw a heavy-set man of about sixty, with shrewd, deep-set eyes staring out from under a massive brow. His hair was white and he didn't seem to have lost any of it. When he laughed, he reminded Edge of a choirboy. He knew the impression was false. Franker had been one of the country's most successful criminal lawyers before he became Prime Minister.

"I've just finished listening to the recording of the speech that Prometheus chap delivered last night," Franker said. "I understand he's in jail."

"He was arrested aboard the Liberty Queen," Hervey said. "According to our intel, he planned to hijack the yacht, and then abduct you and hold you there and force the government's resignation. I think he had plans for a people's parliament. The original plan called for a band of five specially trained guerrillas to do the job, but as you know they were intercepted as they came ashore, so Prometheus X had to attempt the job himself. Fortunately he is a better rabble-rouser than an urban guerrilla."

"And he said he went aboard that yacht to see if there were arms on it for me," Franker said. "Christ! I mean why would I want to bring in arms?"

He turned his brownish-greyish eyes on Edge and Edge wondered how far back in Franker's ancestry it was that some white plantation owner had forced himself on a black woman in a bunch of sugar-cane and started a crop of light-brown Frankers.

"Is that how you see it too, Mr. Edge?"

"That's how it is at the moment," Edge said.

"You expect that to change?" Franker asked him.

"We haven't checked Prometheus X's story yet," Edge said.

Franker looked out the window and his face was expressionless.

"That young man had something," he said. "And there are very few about with anything to offer. I had hoped to harness some of that energy for the use of this country." He frowned suddenly. "But of course that fire wouldn't have lasted anyhow. This society has a way of forcing you into compromises." He turned his eyes on Edge and Hervey. "I had asked him into the Senate once, but he refused. He also refused a seat on one of the statutory boards. My colleagues were horrified. Some thought it was madness. Others called it treason. But I told them I was going to ask him again after the Independence celebrations. We need all the talent we can put our hands on, and we can't afford to have all that energy walking around waiting to be swept up into the wrong cause."

They had another drink and Franker talked about the Independence celebrations, and they left.

Edge watched Hervey unplug the electric kettle and pour water over the tea bag, then add milk and sugar.

"Somebody paid 50 thousand dollars into my account," Edge said.

Hervey put down the teacup. The tea splashed over the rim of the saucer and formed a pool on the desk in front of him.

"You're making me nervous," Hervey said.

"Prometheus X has been set up," Edge said. "And the robbery was never on. Nor was the kidnapping."

"Sure you won't have some tea?" Hervey said.

Edge left the window. He came and stood over Hervey. "Some time tomorrow there's going to be an attempt on Franker's life," he said. "I've been chosen to take the rap."

"That 50 thousand," Hervey said.

"My pay-off. They thought of everything."

"I knew something was wrong," Hervey said. "They threw Prometheus X at us too easily. Travellers cutting loose a horse to distract the wolves." Hervey studied the tips of his fingers. "If Franker gets taken out the Bureau is going to be left holding the can."

"One of the security people has a photograph of myself and Prometheus X talking," Edge said. "A clever lawyer could make something out of it."

"Collusion," Hervey said. He tore open a pack of cigarettes and took one out of the pack.

"They don't know that we know," Edge said.

Hervey pulled the unlit cigarette away from his lips. "Any plans?" he asked.

"I've got to make certain Franker stays alive. I'll need a helicopter."

Hervey glanced up quickly. "I'm not planning to run," Edge said.

Edge put the car in the garage. The back door of the house was open. He slipped the Sauer into his hand. Mrs. Phipps, the housekeeper, came to the door.

"I didn't know you were comin' home so early," she said.

She looked from his face to the gun in his hand. Her expression did not change.

"I thought I'd take an early evening," Edge said. He put up the gun.

She stepped back to let him pass. "I can't come tomorrow," she said. "I want to see the parade. So I decided to come today."

"That's okay."

A child was sitting on the living room floor looking at the pictures in a magazine.

"My last gran," Mrs. Phipps said. "Madge, say good day to the gentleman."

The girl stood up and said formally: "Good day, Sir."

"Call me Shannon," Edge said. "We're friends."

"Yes, Sir," Madge said.

"A Mr. Hercules phoned to tell you to not forget the cricket match tomorrow," Mrs. Phipps said.

He had forgotten the match. He reminded himself to call the captain and tell him he wouldn't be able to play after all. He told her thanks and asked her if she wouldn't like the rest of the day home.

He turned on his stereo and mixed a drink. He drank it quickly, and showered and changed and went out to the car. He saw a Honda Civic in the rear view mirror. It stayed with him for two miles. Edge activated the hands free feature in the Volkswagen and called Hervey.

"All right, who is the joker on my tail?"

"A maverick," Hervey said. "Ditch him."

Edge was silent for a few moments. "Get hold of Meyers," he told Hervey. "Tell him to rent one of those outboard things and meet me off Rockley. And have a car waiting for me in the trees above the Mercado Beach Hotel after dark."

"Will do," Hervey said. "By the way, there is a party this evening in Paradise Heights. If you're looking for some place to cool out, you'll be safe there. Name's Trudy Cricklewood." He gave Edge the directions.

The Civic was not in sight, but he picked up a Mini Clubman about a mile further on. He drove to the beach and parked the car under the trees. He put on his swimming trunks, placed his phone and wallet in a waterproof bag and put the keys in the left front hubcap. The Mini was parked a few yards away. The driver had a worried look on his face.

Edge picked through the sunbathers and the exhibitionists. He dived into the water, turned on his back and floated with the current out beyond the other swimmers and into the dark-blue waters beyond the reef. He closed his eyes and waited for the boat. He heard it. He rolled over and did a long, slow crawl towards the bright speck coming at him out of the afternoon sun. The boat pulled alongside.

"Going my way?" Meyers asked him.

"I was waiting for the Q.E. II, but as you came along I'll go with you instead."

He climbed into the boat and leaned back against the gunwale.

"How's the shoulder?" Meyers asked.

"Coming along fine."

"I brought along something not even the Q.E. II can match," Meyers said.

"Tell me."

"Fishing lines," Meyers said. "I hear there's barracuda around here."

"You're a real comfort," Edge said.

"I try. Anyway it's not barracuda. It's shark. I saw one following you just now. You barely beat it to the boat."

"Shut up," Edge said.

Venus was bright in the western sky when Meyers eased the boat into the shadows. Edge stepped over the side.

"Good luck," Meyers said.

"Thanks. And keep the fish."

He found the car under the trees. He opened the suitcase on the back seat and put on a T-shirt and a pair of jeans. He checked in at the Golden Beach Hotel, went up to his room and fell asleep.

He awoke at nine o'clock. He ordered dinner. He was coming from the shower when the knock sounded at the door. The waiter arranged the trays on the table and went out. He ate dinner. He was almost to the door when he changed his mind about the gun. He went back for it.

Trudy Cricklewood's verandah had coloured lights strung across the front. He parked the car between a Mustang and Mercedes Benz. A woman in an evening gown and a blonde wig was greeting the guests at the top of the steps.

"Edge is the name. Hervey said hello."

"Oh, that old faker," Trudy Cricklewood said. "How's he these days?"

He told her Hervey was fine.

"Glad you made it," she said. "Have a good time."

He went inside. A waiter passed with a tray. He took a beer. Music came softly over the hum of conversation. A few couples were on the floor. The liquor was taking a beating. The music stopped. People drifted away from the centre of the floor. Somebody changed the song on the MP3 player. A woman kicked off her shoes and stood perfectly still in the middle of the floor.

A trumpet cut through the noise and the smoke, clear and crisp and clean as though the notes had been laundered in detergent and hung in the sun to dry. Castanets joined in, chased by bongos and a trombone. Still the woman had not moved. The conversation died. Every eye was on her. She drew her hands slowly down her thighs and the magnificent breasts thrust forward. She raised her left arm above her head. The hand traced circles in the air. The hips began moving counter-clockwise. The arm came down. The hips moved clockwise. A man standing near Edge sucked air noisily through his mouth. His tongue flickered out over his lips.

She raised both arms above her head. Every fourth beat of music, her hips interrupted their circular motion and thrust forward. She picked up the rhythm with her feet. Edge sipped his beer. He was surprised to find his throat dry. A man rushed away from the wall and tried to plant himself in front of the woman. She whirled away and left him.

The music surged towards the climax. Her hands came up cradling her breasts. She dropped her hands and spread her legs. Only the hips moved now, slowly, powerfully, in a rhythmic undulating circle that had every man in the room for its centre. Cymbals crashed. The woman's bottom quivered. She strained against the echoes, her eyes closed.

Bongos tapped out a syncopated roll. A trombone cut in above the percussion. The tension flowed out of the woman's body. She picked up the beat languidly, absently. The music ended on a quiet drum-roll. She sank to the floor with her head between her feet.

Edge rested his glass in the window and joined in the applause. Two men lifted the woman on their shoulders and marched with her around the room. Edge went into the kitchen for another drink. A man was standing near the bar talking to two women.

"Agape, not eros," he was saying. "What Kant called practical love. Love seated in the will. Not that sick condition your hit parade people are always on about."

He caught Edge's eye and he winked. He had kicked off his shoes somewhere. His Afro needed combing. His jeans had tears at the knees. The women were hanging on his every word. He swayed lightly against one of the women. Edge wondered if he was really drunk.

"I was talking about Kant's kind of love," the man said. "Ask any of your average run-of-the-mill rule-agapistic deontologists and see if they don't tell you the same thing."

Edge knew for certain that he was drunk. He winked at Edge again and picked up his drink. The women followed him like the wake behind a battle cruiser. Somebody bumped Edge's elbow. He heard a voice say sorry. He turned. It was the dancer.

"My uncle lives in Corfu," she said.

The Bureau's introduction code for the week. He wasn't ready for it. He had to search his mind for the response.

"You're lucky," he said. "Mine lives in Black Rock."

"This uncle is very rich. He owns boats and things."

Her uncle was rich. That meant she had a message for him, and that it was safe for the two of them to be seen together.

"Tess McCool," she said. "Sorry I spilled your drink."

"What are you having?"

"I'll have the rum punch, if there's any left."

Edge went and got the rum punch. She threaded her arm through his and they went out on to the verandah.

"When was the last time you saw Shelley Hardcastle?" Tess asked.

"Yesterday. Why?"

"She sleeps with a Cabinet Minister."

Edge waited.

"The Honourable Mervin Steele."

Edge drank some of his beer. Tess put her hand on his arm. She said: "Mr. Hervey said you were in love with her. I'm sorry."

Edge smiled. That would be Hervey's idea of a joke, he thought.

"How did you come to work for Hervey?"

"I used to be a party-girl," Tess said. "I would go out with important people, help them to relax and keep my eyes and ears open." She drank some of the rum punch. "I also run a beauty salon," she continued. "You'd be surprised the things I hear. I was told to try to get next to Hervey, but somehow I ended up working for him. I never could figure out just how he managed it."

She put down her glass. "I used to be Mervin Steele's woman," she said. "Before that plantation bitch got her hooks into him. He would never have married me. I know that. I'm not rich enough, or important enough. But he used to come around every night, and I liked that. He never comes anymore." She laughed and Edge heard the bittersweet echoes of love gone sour.

"Who was your case-officer before Hervey turned you?"

"I used to get my instructions from one of the little Parliamentary Secretaries. They call them 'Parl-Secs' I think."

Edge put his hands on her shoulders and pulled her to him. She gave a little start of surprise and her mouth was working against his.

"Get your things," he said. "We're leaving."

"This party isn't even warm yet." She was smiling.

"Yeah. I know."

He found Trudy Cricklewood dancing with a man who looked young enough to be her son. Edge told her it was a lovely party. She told him to drop by again some time.

They had been driving for about ten minutes. He stopped the car and turned off the lights. He waited five minutes. He started the car and drove without lights until he saw a gap. He turned the car. He switched on the lights and drove back towards the house. The road was still empty.

He picked up the coast road further on. He stopped the car on the hill and sat watching the starlight bounce off the phosphorescence in the water. He slipped the car into gear and drove down to the beach.

"You can't make up your mind which side I'm on," she said. "You don't know how to take me."

He turned towards her. "How should I take you?"

"Naked, preferably."

She began to take her clothes off.

Chapter 13

Eagle In The Sky

The lizard came out of the tall grass and raised itself high on its legs and swung its head from side to side. Edge leaned against the trunk of the sugar-apple tree and watched. The lizard flattened itself against the ground and Edge knew it had seen food. A grasshopper leaped a few yards away, and the lizard darted forward and its jaws closed around the soft green body. The lizard dived into the grass. One of the grasshopper's legs was lying on the ground.

The helicopter came in low over the sugarcane. He stood up and waved. The helicopter came down a few yards away. The door opened and he climbed in.

"There's sandwiches and coffee behind you." It was Meyers.

"Jesus! Am I glad to see you!" Edge said. He left the sandwiches and the coffee where they were.

"Where did you learn to handle these things?" he asked Meyers.

"A two-week stint with the coast guard," Meyers said. "I used to hit trees and house-tops, but I haven't hit any recently."

"I was only asking. I'm glad you're here."

"Glad to see you too," Meyers said. "Brought a couple of automatic rifles. And there's enough gas in this thing to get us to St. Lucia."

"Somebody's been gossiping."

"Heard somebody's got our ass in a sling."

"You told Hervey about the guns?"

"No, but I figured we might have to shoot our way out if Franker gets hit."

"We've got one little thing going for us," Edge said.

"Buddy, everything we got going for us can be stuck up a mosquito's ass and he would still be able to fart hard," Meyers said.

"They don't know we know," Edge said. "And as long as it remains that way, we have a chance."

"Are you saying you're sticking with this shit?"

"I don't like clever people," Edge said. "Particularly I don't like clever people who try to set me up. Somebody put 50 thousand dollars in my account, so you can be certain there's enough evidence to prove I had something to do with Franker being hit." He took the Sauer out, checked the magazine and rammed home the clip. "No. I've got to make sure that Franker keeps breathing."

"Let's split while we have a chance," Meyers said.

"How far do you think we'd get? No, it has to be this way."

"Look, we can go to the police. Give ourselves up. We can't take anybody out if we're in custody."

"They'd love that," Edge said. "Shot while trying to escape and nobody would ask them one question."

Meyers sighed. "My mother always said I'd come to a bad end," he said. He spoke into the microphone. "Eagle calling Control. Eagle calling Control!"

Hervey acknowledged. Meyers told him he and Edge were going to do some looking around.

The sugar-cane was behind them and they were low over one of the residential areas, the ones real estate developers called 'gardens'; an expensive, exclusive ghetto with no pavements and no place for children to play. Whoever laid it out, had done so as though they expected the landscape to conform to the houses eventually. It reminded Edge of pus running down a good looking leg.

"Franker is using a double this morning," Meyers said. "At least until he gets to the parade. A car with a stand-in and a policewoman who looks like his wife will take the route that was advertised. Franker will travel by unmarked car using another route."

The Prime Minister's residence came into view behind a screen of trees. The motorcycle escort swept through the gate followed by the official car. The helicopter followed the procession for about five minutes, then Meyers did a ninety-degree turn off to the left.

"Come around again," Edge said. He had the binoculars to his eyes.

Meyers brought the machine round in a tight turn.

"Somebody's on the roof over there," he pointed. "See that old building?"

Below them, the road curved sharply then climbed for about half a mile. The derelict building stood near the corner. There were two men on the roof. They were looking out over the road. One of them was adjusting the sights of a rifle. The other was following the progress of the official party through a pair of binoculars. It was the flash of the sun on the binoculars that had alerted Edge.

The helicopter came in from the opposite direction. The outriders approached the corner. The man behind the rifle pressed his eye against the telescopic sights. The man with the binoculars dropped them suddenly and rolled over. He came up on his knees with a rifle in his hands. Edge shouted a warning to Meyers. Meyers had already seen the man. The helicopter swerved and banked. Edge rested the barrel of the Sauer against his forearm. Flame winked from the rifle in the man's hand and he staggered upright and the rifle fell from his hands and four small holes appeared in the Perspex glass near Edge's head.

"They were waiting for us," Meyers said. "They knew we were coming."

Edge was already swinging down from the hovering machine. He dropped the last few feet and he went off balance and he heard the whistle of a bullet past his ear. He kept rolling and the pain tore through his shoulder, and he bit down hard against the agony and shot twice from flat on his stomach. The man came upright. He took two short steps forward and fell on his face.

Rubbing his sore shoulder, Edge dropped down behind the rifle. He picked up the procession in the crosshairs. He swung the rifle and held Franker's stand-in in his sights. As the car pulled away up the hill, Edge thought perhaps, a crack, international-class assassin might get in two shots before the car accelerated out of danger.

The gun was a Lee Enfield 303, a slow noisy weapon, altogether unsuited for a high precision assassination job.

Edge climbed back into the helicopter. Neither man said anything. The helicopter soared over the cane fields as Edge contacted Hervey through his headset.

"Eagle calling Control."

"Come in Eagle," Hervey said.

"Two men were waiting for the procession," Edge said. "They took a shot at us. Get somebody out there quick."

"I'm glad it's over." Hervey's voice was heavy with relief. Are you coming in? Franker has already arrived."

"I'll stay out a bit longer," Edge said.

"Hold on," Hervey said quickly. "I think Cooper's trying to say something." Edge waited. Hervey came on again. "You might want to take a run over to the radio station," Hervey said. "Somebody just threw a bomb at it."

Meyers brought the helicopter down on the lawn in front of the radio station. Edge climbed out and walked over to the group of policemen standing in the yard. They turned and watched him approach. Even from that distance he could sense their bewilderment. The sergeant drew himself up straight.

"Morning sergeant," Edge said. "What happened?"

"It appears that someone threw a bomb on the roof of the building," the sergeant said. "We're investigating."

He was a large man with sad eyes and a great, drooping moustache. He looked hurt, as though nobody had ever told him what to do if someone ever tried to blow up the radio station, and he thought it very unfair.

"You've told the announcers not to put it on the air," Edge said.

The sergeant said yes he had and Edge saw his face brighten. But Edge knew the staff would already have been on the phone to everybody they could think of, or posted the event on social media.

The sergeant took him to see the damage. The bomb had blown a hole in the roof and ceiling and scattered pieces of wood and plaster over the receptionist's desk.

"I've sent the cap and piece of the fuse to the lab for examination," the sergeant said.

"Anybody saw anything suspicious?" Edge asked.

"Nobody ain't seen nothing," the sergeant said.

"I'm sure you did your best," Edge said.

The sergeant said thanks, but the worried look was back in his eyes. He grasped his eighteen-inch cane tighter.

Meyers was standing beside the helicopter waiting for Edge.

"If that bomb had been thrown through a window or planted inside, people would have been killed and the station would have been wrecked," Edge said.

"Okay so they got scared. Or they missed."

Edge shook his head. "No. Somebody was merely softening up the public. The bomb wasn't meant to blow up the station."

Meyers rubbed the tip of his chin with his fingers. "I suppose you're going to tell me the men on the roof were put there to draw the helicopter out into the open and that the ambush was a blind?"

"They had glasses," Edge said. "And they saw us before we saw them. They were looking at us through the glasses when we spotted them. They let us get up close and then tried to shoot us down. We're up against pros and pros don't use obsolete weapons at two hundred yards in an assassination caper. They prefer cross-fires with fast, modern equipment."

"That means that Franker is still under the gun," Meyers said.

They got into the helicopter and watched the ground drop away below.

Edge leaned back and closed his eyes. "Tell me about the new security arrangements for the parade," he said.

"The place is sewn up tighter than a drum. Nobody can get within fifty yards of Franker without tripping over a dozen security men." He took out a packet of cigarettes and lit one. "The only things that haven't been moved back, are the saluting base and the flag that will be flying above Franker's head while he takes the salute."

Edge sat up and opened his eyes. Suddenly, he knew how Franker was going to die.

Hervey said: "Control here. Come in Eagle."

"How far away is the march-past?" Edge asked.

"About five minutes," Hervey said.

"Stop it. Stop the march-past."

"Did I hear you say stop the march-past?"

"You did."

"Nobody can stop a march-past," Hervey said.

"Okay. I'm coming in. Warn Cooper."

Meyers brought the helicopter in low over the crowded Garrison grandstand. Edge saw the upturned faces and some people waving. Women in large hats and elbow length gloves clutched at their hats and beat at their skirts to keep them down. They swooped over the public area and above the heads of the members of the Barbados Defense

Force, who were drawn up in a column of route awaiting orders from the Commanding Officer.

The helicopter came down in an open area beyond the saluting base. The band swung into 'Scipio'. Edge jumped out of the helicopter and sprinted towards Franker who was standing on the saluting base. Members of the Barbados Defense Force and a few security men looked on, wondering what was taking place. Franker stood like a wax figure in a museum except that little rivulets of sweat were coursing down his face.

"Mr. Prime Minister," Edge said quietly. "You're standing on a bomb."

"What?" Franker asked.

A woman screamed in the VIP enclosure. Over in the public area there was a sudden stirring like sheep sensing danger. Franker looked at Edge.

"You're standing on a bomb," Edge said again.

Franker just stood there. Edge took his hand and pulled him off the saluting base. He ran, dragging Franker with him. Edge shouted orders at the security men who were nearby. They ran from the area as well.

Edge sensed that the music had stopped, and that sounds of confusion had broken out behind him. The earth shook. An explosion ripped the saluting-base apart. Edge and the Prime Minister were thrown to the ground. The force of the explosion made Edge's senses spin. A cloud of debris whirled above the saluting-base and fell back to earth. The dust settled. The echoes faded. Edge stood up. Franker climbed to his knees, slipped and fell back. Edge bent and brought him upright and held him steady. Franker's knees buckled. His jaw hung slack. His head swung aimlessly on the thick neck, and suddenly his clothes seemed several sizes too big for him. He glanced down at his hands.

"I-I-I just don't know what to say," he croaked. "I guess I owe you my life."

Cooper's men planted in the crowd began cheering. Other people picked it up. The cheering spread and the crowd began channeling its tension into nervous applause.

Franker reacted to the applause like an old warhorse hearing a bugle. The glazed look left his eyes gradually. He drew himself slowly up to his full height. He stood like a rock in the surf while the waves of applause washed over him.

Cooper raced across the grass towards them. Franker waited until he was close.

"Tell the band to start playing again," he said.

"Yes, Mr. Prime Minister," Cooper said.

Edge walked to the helicopter. He studied the officials' enclosure through the glasses. He lowered the glasses and got in beside Meyers.

"We've got another stop to make," he said.

He gave Meyers the address. Meyers lit a cigarette and took the machine into the air. They came down in the back of the house behind the orchard. Edge climbed down and scaled the wall and went through the trees. A dog barked somewhere inside the house. Edge slipped the Sauer into his hand. The garage was open. Edge crouched down behind the Audi and waited. Footsteps came across the yard. Edge heard the car door open. He stood up.

"Hello Mervin," he said. "Not leaving us I hope."

Steele's mouth opened and closed, but no sound came. Edge showed him the gun.

"Stop pointing that thing at me," Steele said.

Two suitcases were on the ground beside him. He wore a dark-blue suit and black shoes and he carried a grey overcoat.

"End of play," Edge said. "You had your innings."

Steele regained his composure with an effort of will that brought perspiration to his brow.

"Is this your idea of a game?" he said coldly. "May I remind you that you could find yourself in serious trouble?"

"The head-prefect bit isn't going to work, you know."

Steele made one more try. "Get out of my way," he said. "I've got serious business to attend to."

"They're going to hang you. You know that."

Steele's shoulders drooped. "I saw your performance on the television," he said. He seemed to make up his mind suddenly. "How much do you want?" he asked. "You can name your figure."

Edge shook his head. "I'm not for sale," he said.

"I see. You've come to murder me."

A dog came out of the house. It stopped a little way off and watched the two men. Steele smiled. He took a step back. His breath whistled past his teeth in an explosive rush.

A savage growl was the only warning Edge got. One moment the dog was standing there looking at them, the next, the brute was streaking at him. He had time for one shot. Two, if he shot really fast. But there wasn't much of a target. The dog was coming at him too fast and too close to the ground.

Edge braced himself and squeezed the trigger. The dog kept coming. Christ! He must've missed. He saw the slavering jaws, saw the muscles bunch as the dog gathered itself to spring, then the spring turned into a long slide and the dog did the final few feet on its belly and came to rest with its muzzle against Edge's shoes.

Steele looked from Edge to the dog. Tears came to his eyes. He knelt beside the dog's body and he looked at Edge again. "You killed Charlemagne," he said.

Edge wiped the sweat from his forehead. His knees were shaking. He lowered the gun till it was pointing to the ground.

Steele straightened up. His eyes were smoldering behind the steel rimmed glasses.

"Letting you live was our biggest mistake," Steele said.

Edge shrugged. "Not that you didn't try," he said. "Twice, if I remember right. It wasn't until you failed that you and your cohorts picked me to take the drop for Franker's killing."

He lifted the gun and pointed it at Steele's middle. He felt a sudden weariness. Steele was calmer now, as though he had reached some vital decision and the rest did not matter. Edge studied the face of the man he had known since boyhood and who now stared back at him across a chasm neither of them could bridge. What had happened, he wondered. What had gone wrong? Some of the anger, the disappointment, and the sense of betrayal he felt showed in his face. He saw Steele wince.

"I never thought you were one of Franker's supporters," Steele said tightly. "Yet there you were, risking your life to save his. Unexpected but touching nevertheless." He shook his head. "Don't expect gratitude from Franker," he continued. "I know that man."

Edge could have told him it had nothing to do with Franker. He had accepted a job and he would do it to the limits of his capacity. And when he felt he could no longer do it, for whatever reason, he would walk away from it, even if it meant driving a truck, or diving sea-eggs for the rest of his days. He could have told Steele all this, but he could not see the purpose it would serve. Instead, he asked Steele the question that was bothering him.

"Why?"

Steele drew a slow deep breath. His eyes wandered beyond Edge and focused on the blue emptiness in the distance.

"This country belongs to the man big enough to take it," he said. "I almost got there. I almost took it from Franker's flabby hands." He was talking to himself now. "Franker is a bleeding-heart liberal and Prometheus X is a Communist. This country can't afford either." He drew his hands slowly across his face. "So close," he said. "I came so very near."

"The trial will be an unpleasant business," Edge said. "The car would be easier."

Steele raised his eyes. Edge saw resolution harden in them. "Yes," he said. "The car. I agree with you. That way I won't have the vulgar crowd baying at my heels." He tried to smile. "It is after all," he continued, "the manner of dying rather than the manner of living that marks the man."

"I wouldn't know," Edge said. "I suppose there'll be a state funeral. The people will go delirious with grief. With any luck, your colleagues will name a street or a school after you."

Marvin Steele glanced down at the two suitcases. "I'll need a couple of minutes to unpack," he said.

He came back in five minutes. He paused at the top of the steps as though fixing the memory in his mind. He adjusted his glasses, squared his shoulders and walked to the car.

"I'm sorry about the car," he said. "It's a beautiful car." He turned towards Edge. "Oh," he said. "You can tell Franker it was nothing personal."

Edge watched him back out of the garage and drive through the gate. He walked back to the helicopter.

"Did I hear shooting or was somebody setting off firecrackers?" Meyers asked.

Edge climbed in and sat down. He didn't answer. He leaned back in his seat and closed his eyes. Meyers took the helicopter into the air.

"Where to?" he asked.

Edge reached for the binoculars and searched the roads below them. He picked out the silver Audi easily among the sparse mid-morning traffic. He tapped Meyers on the shoulder and showed him the car.

"Keep it in sight," he said.

"If he's leaving the country, he's going the wrong way," Meyers said. "The airport's in the opposite direction."

"He's leaving the country all right," Edge said. "But not from the airport."

The car approached a left hand curve. It was going too fast. It drifted to the opposite side, skidded back into the centre of the road, fought for a grip on the asphalt, won, and thundered on up the highway, smoke pouring from its exhausts. Meyers let his breath out in a long, slow whistle. He had not been aware that he had stopped breathing. Edge wondered which spot Steele had chosen and what he was thinking as he gunned the car on.

The road twisted along the side of a hill, and the sea below the cliff sparkled in the morning sun.

"I don't think we're going to raise him," Meyers said.

The corner was sharp and narrow and by this time Steele had taken the car up beyond a hundred. He missed the corner. The car whipped across the road and sliced through the safety barrier and went over the cliff. The doors burst open. A doll-like figure sailed clear. The car ploughed through boulders and stunted bushes, tumbled over and over and rolled down to the beach and came to rest on the sand with the wheels in the air. A huge boulder, shaken loose from its mooring, followed the path gouged out by the car and rolled slowly down into the water.

"Sweet Jesus Christ," Meyers breathed.

Flames licked the edges of the wreck. The wind came in off the sea and the fire spread. An explosion ripped the gas tank open. A column of flame shot into the air and thick, oily smoke spread above the flames.

"I guess you could say Steele made quite an impact on this country of ours," Meyers said.

Edge turned towards him. Meyers saw the look on his face.

"I know," Meyers said. "I talk too much."

A car stopped on the road below. A man and a woman got out. The man started climbing down to the beach.

"I think perhaps we'd better be getting back," Edge said.

Chapter 14

Down-Beat

Hervey said: "Hill and his man Trask have been deported. Cooper hauled them in for questioning. Hill screamed for the Ambassador. Cooper let him go. Insufficient evidence."

He oscillated his pen between his thumb and forefinger and nodded at Edge across the desk. "I'm trying to finish this report," he said. "The Prime Minister wants it tonight."

"I hear he cried when he heard about Steele," Edge said.

"Steele was his protégé. They say Franker was grooming him as his successor."

Edge pushed back his chair. "Good luck with the report," he said.

Christ he was tired. He listened absently to the sound of the rain on the windowpanes. The clock on the wall behind Hervey was saying ten. He wondered if the radio station was still playing solemn music. Steele's death had brought celebrations to an end. Flags had dropped to half-mast and all official functions had been cancelled.

"Goodnight," Hervey said. "Try not to fall asleep at the wheel."

Edge went out to the car. The rain had stopped but clouds still hid the stars. Cooper was in his office. He looked up from his papers in front of him and frowned at Edge.

"Don't you ever sleep?"

"Tell me about Thomas Bunker Hill and his man Trask."

"They left earlier this evening."

"I know that. I mean about him and Steele.'

"Don't you ever give up?"

Edge dropped into the chair across from Cooper and waited.

"I can give you what I know," Cooper said. "Franker refused to move against Prometheus X, so Steele decided to move against Franker. Steele made an arrangement with Hill. Hill would get exclusive rights to any oil found on the island and in return would get his friends in Congress to drum up support for the Steele government." Cooper rubbed his fingers into the stubble under his chin.

"You got in the way," he continued. "When they couldn't kill you, they arranged it in such a way that Prometheus X and his people would be blamed for Franker's murder and you would appear to be implicated."

"Where would Steele get support for a caper like that?"

"You're testing out your theories on me again," Cooper said.

"Just comparing ideas," Edge said.

Cooper shrugged, and looked up at Edge. "Support for the idea would be no problem. This country prides itself on being conservative. Some would say reactionary. Our lunatic fringe begins in the middle and moves both ways."

"One more thing. You knew I was being set up."

"I decided to let you handle it," Cooper said. "If you were really as good as you were said to be, then you wouldn't need any help. Look, I've got four children at school and would like to make Commissioner before I retire, and maybe even become Consul General in New York afterwards."

Edge did not laugh. Cooper leaned towards him. "I'll do anything for a friend but I won't stick my neck out. See those tall straight casuarina trees we got around here? Most of us are like them. Straight. Except when you look close, they're not really straight, they're leaning away at an angle. That's because of the pressure of the wind. If they don't lean away, they break. Most of us are like that." He jabbed a finger into Edge's chest. "You don't lean away, but we all can't be like you. Now go away and let me work."

Edge stood up. "You're a fairly all right son-of-a-bitch," he said. "I appreciate the help you gave me."

They shook hands.

Edge drove slowly through the wet, empty streets. The policeman on guard outside Steele's house stepped out of the shadows and stood in the beam of the headlights. Edge showed his identification. The policeman waved him on. He parked the car and went up the steps. Another shadow came towards him across the verandah.

"Evening sergeant," Edge said.

The man hesitated. Edge could almost hear him wondering what to do. Edge took a bunch of keys from his pocket and unlocked the door.

"Come in out of the cold, sergeant," he said.

"I don't understand this," the sergeant said.

"Call Assistant Commissioner Cooper if you have any questions," Edge said.

The man followed him into the house. Edge switched on the lights. The furniture was early 1900's New England. There was a chrome and mahogany cocktail bar against the wall. The wall-to-wall carpet looked very expensive.

Edge went into the bedrooms. The beds were made and the room tidied. Edge wondered idly if Steele had done it himself or if the maid had been in. The photograph he was looking for was on one of the dressing-tables. He removed it from the frame and put it in his pocket. He was putting the empty frame back when the saw the note. He picked it up and read it.

"I have not loved the world nor the world me.
I have not flattered its rank breath nor bowed
To its idolatries a patient knee
Nor coined my cheek to smiles: nor cried aloud
In worship of an echo. In the crowd
They could not deem me one of such, I stood

Amongst them, but not of them: in a shroud
Of thoughts that were not their thoughts, and still could
Had I not 'filed my mind, which thus itself subdued."

Edge read it through a second time. Under the bombast and the lofty claims was the usual unspoken admission of moral failure and of ideals betrayed. Edge had heard it before. And he had known many Mervin Steeles, little men with shrunken souls and soaring ambitions. They were special people and anxious to prove it. Listen to them and they'll tell you why they and they alone are the final bulwark against creeping cant and philistinism. Flatter them and they'll reward you with their gratitude. Cultivate their egos and they'll connive at murder.

He folded the piece of paper and put it back. He switched off the light and went out.

"I need a drink," he told the sergeant. "Feel like one?"

"Rum and coke," the sergeant said.

Edge poured straight rum for himself. The sergeant tasted his drink.

"Nice place this," he said. There was awe in his voice. "A pity about the accident. Barbados lost a good man."

"You know what they say about the good," Edge said. "They die young."

He walked to the window, took out his phone and called Shelley Hardcastle. He came back and turned off the lights.

Lights were on in the Hardcastle house. He pushed the door. It was unlocked.

"Anybody home?"

"In here. Come on through," Shelley said.

Edge followed the sound of her voice. The bedroom door was open. He heard running water.

"Is that you Shannon?" Shelley called. "I'll be out in a minute."

Edge went back out to the sideboard. He poured rum into a glass and came back. When Shelley came out of the bath, he was leaning against the door with the drink in his hand. She smiled at him.

"Did you pour one for me?"

She took the glass from him. She took a sip and made a face and handed the glass back to him. Edge looked at her a long time. She was a very lovely woman. She wore a knee-length, gold-coloured robe belted low over the hips. Her face glowed from vigorous scrubbing. She smelled of cologne and bath-oil and other exciting things.

"What will you have?" he asked her.

"Scotch and soda."

He brought the drink. They stood close together, touching. She looked into his eyes and her head fell on his chest.

"I was afraid you weren't ever coming back," she said.

"I promised I would. Remember?"

"Yes, you did. But I still wondered."

"I got something to tell you."

"Don't make it too long," Shelley said. "You and I have other things to do."

She went to the bed and sat down arranging her feet carefully under her. Edge picked up an aerosol can of hair spray from the dressing table and studied the contents of the label. Shelley smiled uncertainly above the rim of her glass.

"Remember Mervin Steele?" Edge said. He shook the can. It sounded about half-full. "He wanted to be a king or something like it. He raised his own little band of angels, and tried to kill Franker and start an empire of his own. Steele died in his car this morning."

"Why are you bothering to tell me all this?" Shelley asked.

"You and Charles were part of it," Edge said. "The men who went overseas for training were friends of Charles. You set me up at the Lilly Pad. When that didn't work you led me to your brother so that he could tell me how the wicked followers of Prometheus X had infiltrated the cultural club and planned a revolution." He put the can of hairspray down on the dressing table. "But you wouldn't know anything about that, would you now, Angel Eyes?"

Shelley shook her head. Pain and disbelief showed on her face.

"You can't mean what you're saying." She put her glass on the bedside-table and stood up. She moved towards Edge. She tugged gently at her robe to reveal more of her cleavage. "We haven't got anything to fight about," she said.

Edge embraced her and she kissed him. "What's past is past."

"Wrong," Edge said. "The past is never really behind us. We carry it with us every minute of our lives." But he was smiling.

Shelley tilted her head back and ran her fingers through her hair. She closed her eyes. "Come and make love to me," she said. A pulse beat at the base of her throat. She moaned softly.

A muscle at the corner of her mouth twitched just as the arm flashed. Edge was ready. He chopped against Shelley's forearm with the side of his hand. The knife flew across the room. She clawed at his eyes. Edge pushed her to the floor.

"You son-of-a-bitch," she screamed.

Edge picked up the knife and threw it in a corner. He took the photograph from his pocket and tossed it into her lap.

"He would have wanted you to have this back," he said.

"I loved him," Shelley said. "And I would have done anything for him. Can you understand something like that? I loved him." She began to cry.

"Tell Charles to come out," Edge said. "He can't hide behind your skirts forever."

"I'm here." The voice came from behind Edge. "Turn around. Slowly. And keep your hands where I can see them."

Edge turned. Charles Hardcastle stood in the doorway. He had a gun in his hand.

"Steele had more sense," Edge said. "He killed himself."

Hardcastle smiled. There was a look of amused contempt in his eyes. The gun in his hand was as steady as a rocket launcher.

"The gun," he said. "Lift it out with two fingers and drop it in front of you."

Edge took out the gun and dropped it on the carpet.

"Now kick it away to your left," Hardcastle said.

Edge kicked the gun away. Hardcastle said: "You shouldn't have come here. That was most unwise."

"I came here to kill you."

"So! Franker's hatchet-man to the last, eh?"

"No. This is personal."

"Personal?"

Edge picked up his glass and sipped his drink. "A kid I knew took a bomb that was meant for me. He wanted to be a Test cricketer and racecar driver and a few other things. He probably would have wound up like the rest of us scrambling for enough food to live. But now, we'll never know. I think I owe him something.

"You'll have me crying in a minute."

That's the trouble with amateurs, Edge thought. You talk too much. The pros hit first and make the speeches after. He put down his glass. His eyes never left Hardcastle's face.

"The gun won't change anything," Edge said. "We already have all the evidence we need."

"My idea sounds better." Hardcastle laughed. "I heard a scream. I rushed in here and saw my sister struggling with a man and I shot him. Family honour and all that, you know. I'm sorry, but you're already dead."

Edge said wearily: "You tell him, Meyers."

The colour drained from Hardcastle's face. He swung his head slightly. It was pure reflex and he recovered swiftly, but Edge had already hurled the container of hairspray and was diving for the Sauer.

Hardcastle's gun sounded like thunder. Something zipped past Edge's ear and there was a warm breath on his cheek. The dive took him within inches of the Sauer. He kept on rolling. His fingers clawed for the gun. It seemed half-a-mile away. Edge knew Hardcastle couldn't miss with his next shot.

The floor shook under him. There was a flash of blinding white light. The carpet tasted bitter and gritty. He waited for the pain.

He was screaming. The screams were inside his head. He opened his eyes. He spat out a mouthful of carpet-fibre. The screams were louder.

Edge got up off of the floor. Hardcastle lay on his back near the door. Half his face was blown away. He was drumming his heels against the carpet like an animal with its head caught in a trap.

Edge saw a sliver of tin on the carpet. It was black and twisted, as though it had been in a fire. He glanced at the thing on the floor again. He felt his stomach heave. He looked away. Hardcastle's bullet had hit the container and it had exploded in his face. Edge went across the room to Shelley. She was on the floor. She seemed unhurt. Edge had his phone in his hand.

"Send an ambulance over to the Hardcastle house," he said.

"I put one on standby ever since you left," Hervey said.

"So you knew about Hardcastle then?"

"I was guessing just like you."

"I'll leave you to get on with your report."

"Are you all right?"

"Yeah. I'm okay."

"I'm glad it's over," Hervey said. The weariness was coming through. "And by the way," he continued. "You are a very tough son-of-a-bitch. Sleep well."

Edge wondered how much the effort had cost Hervey.

"I'll see you in a couple of days," he said.

Hardcastle's whimper followed him down the steps. The sound of thunder came to him over the breeze. He stood at the bottom of the steps and filled his lungs with the clean night air. The rain felt cool and fresh on his face. He reminded himself to draw the 50 thousand from his account first thing in the morning and give it to Greene's mother.

Edge watched the funeral on television. The cathedral was full. People spilled into the yard outside. Some of them were crying. Franker and the Cabinet sat in the front pews. The country's leading soprano sang 'O Rest In the Lord'. The band of the Royal Barbados Police played 'Panis Angelicus'. A trumpet section of the Barbados Defence Force played 'Last Post'.

Five priests from five different denominations shared the service. The Dean delivered the oration. He walked slowly to the microphones arranging his robes over his shoulders like Laurence Olivier addressing the Roman Senate. He said: "The beauty of Israel is slain upon its high places." Edge turned off the set.

He poured himself another drink. It was hot and bright outside. The clouds that had hung low on the horizon all morning were now hurrying in from the sea, driven by a strong east wind.

Fenella appeared in the doorway. "How many of those things did you have?" she asked.

"I stopped counting after seven," Edge said.

"Is there any room left for dinner?"

Edge stood up. He bent and swung her off her feet and carried her to the table. He pulled out a chair with his foot and sat her down at the table. She had cooked chicken-beef-and-pork pelau in coconut milk.

THE END

Carl Jackson was born in Barbados where he attended Providence Boys' and Boys' Foundation schools. He is a graduate of Oxford University in England and Ryerson University in Toronto. He is a retired Foreign Service Officer who was stationed in Europe, Canada and the Caribbean.

On his return to Barbados from Ryerson, he was a columnist for the island's two leading newspapers. After Mr. Jackson retired from the Foreign Service, he founded a public relations company where he worked extensively with political parties in Barbados and the Eastern Caribbean.

In 1981, Mr. Jackson published his first novel, *East Wind in Paradise*. His background in journalism, as well as in regional politics played a major part in the creation of this political thriller whose plot and characters are just as relevant today as they were when the novel was first published.

Edge: East Wind in Paradise brings Mr. Jackson's original novel into the 21st century without compromising his themes, characters and crisp writing style.

Made in the USA
Charleston, SC
14 November 2014